As her knees started to buckle against him . . .

. . . she looped her arms around his neck and said, "My place . . . it's right down the street . . . please." He raised his head to look into her eyes, and whatever he saw there seemed to give him the answer he was seeking.

Jason disentangled them enough to walk and said, "Ride with me. Your car will be safe here." Way past any rational thought, she allowed him to lead her over to his Mercedes and put her in the passenger seat, and within minutes they were pulling into her apartment complex. He hurried around the car and helped her out. Her fingers were shaking too much to find the door key, so she handed the whole set to him. He gave a shout of victory as he finally located the key, and soon they were inside.

When the door closed, he reached for her and brought his lips crashing down on hers again. Gone was the questioning kiss of before; now there was only need and desire so hot that she was afraid she would burst into flames. . . .

WEEKENDS
REQUIRED

A DANVERS NOVEL

SYDNEY LANDON

A SIGNET BOOK

SIGNET
Published by New American Library, a division of
Penguin Group (USA) Inc., 375 Hudson Street,
New York, New York 10014, USA
Penguin Group (Canada), 90 Eglinton Avenue East, Suite 700, Toronto,
Ontario M4P 2Y3, Canada (a division of Pearson Penguin Canada Inc.)
Penguin Books Ltd., 80 Strand, London WC2R 0RL, England
Penguin Ireland, 25 St. Stephen's Green, Dublin 2,
Ireland (a division of Penguin Books Ltd.)
Penguin Group (Australia), 707 Collins Street, Melbourne, Victoria 3008,
Australia (a division of Pearson Australia Group Pty. Ltd.)
Penguin Books India Pvt. Ltd., 11 Community Centre, Panchsheel Park,
New Delhi–110 017, India
Penguin Group (NZ), 67 Apollo Drive, Rosedale, Auckland 0632,
New Zealand (a division of Pearson New Zealand Ltd.)
Penguin Books, Rosebank Office Park, 181 Jan Smuts Avenue,
Parktown North 2193, South Africa
Penguin China, B7 Jaiming Center, 27 East Third Ring Road North,
Chaoyang District, Beijing 100020, China

Penguin Books Ltd., Registered Offices:
80 Strand, London WC2R 0RL, England

Published by Signet, an imprint of New American Library,
a division of Penguin Group (USA) Inc.

First Signet Printing, January 2013
10 9 8 7 6 5 4 3 2 1

Ⓟ REGISTERED TRADEMARK—MARCA REGISTRADA

Printed in the United States of America

ALWAYS LEARNING   PEARSON

This book is dedicated to my husband, the man who makes me believe in fairy tales and happily ever after each day. This would not have been possible without his support and encouragement.

Also to my mother: No matter what the idea, she's always completely on board and has never said that it couldn't be done. She is the support system and cheerleader of the family.

Chapter One

"Holy smoking buns, a butt like his should be illegal." Claire looked up in time to see the object of her co-worker and best friend's admiration walk past their table in the cafeteria. Jason Danvers truly did have a butt to admire. At well over six feet tall with dark brown hair that tended to curl up at the ends, compelling ice-blue eyes that looked right through you and a rugged and tanned, athletic build, Jason Danvers was very hard to ignore. His presence always seemed to dominate a room. His every movement impatient, Jason never seemed to relax. Every lady in the cafeteria was craning her neck to get a better look.

"Suzy, keep it down before Mr. Smoking Buns hears you."

"Oh, puleeze. Don't tell me the drool isn't pooling in your mouth as we speak."

"Suz, you're too much—what's Jeff going to do with you?"

"Well, I don't know what Jeff has in mind, but I've

got thoughts of handcuffs and whipped cream, myself."

Claire had met Suzy on her first day at Danvers International, and it hadn't taken long to form a bond with the outspoken, flashy, and hopelessly sex-obsessed wisecracker. Suzy was what every little girl wanted to grow up to be: gorgeous and confident. With long dark red hair, a tall, slim build with curves in all the right places, Suzy loved pushing the fashion envelope at the office. She handled special events for Danvers International and, as she often told anyone who would listen, she was damn good at her job.

Her boss had long ago given up trying to stress the importance of the professional dress code to her and now suffered in silence when Suzy showed up for work in various forms of leather and lace or neon-colored T-shirts with catchy slogans. Claire suspected that Suzy was so beautiful that no one actually cared what she wore, as long as they could admire her every day.

Claire considered today to be a subdued day for Suzy, wearing only a blue-jean miniskirt and a rainbow-colored shirt with a peace sign on it. She often wondered how they'd bonded so quickly. Suzy had a colorful and sexy fashion style, to say the least. Claire preferred a more tailored look. Classic slacks and tops or pencil skirts in neutral tones were her usual work attire. Whereas Suzy favored I've-just-had-hot-sex hair, Claire's tresses were long, auburn, and tended to curl when loose, so for the most part she kept her hair pulled back from her face in a discreet ponytail.

Suzy also loved the tanning salons, even though Claire often lectured her on the dangers of that particular pastime. Wherever they went, men stopped to stare at Suzy, and Claire might as well be a picture on the wall or a potted plant for all the attention they paid to her. Suzy always begged Claire to let her do a makeover. Claire shuddered at the thought.

"I don't know how you work so closely with him without attacking him."

"I value my job, and I just don't think of him in that way—or any man for that matter right now."

"You're way too uptight. Live a little, Claire. You might actually enjoy it."

Thankfully, Suzy seemed to run out of steam in a relatively short time with her "live a little" pep talk, and packed up her tray. "Want to catch a movie later or check out the new bar on the corner?" Suzy asked.

"I've got to run over to Mom's to pay her bills for the month."

"One day you're going to have a wild moment, and I hope I'm still young enough to appreciate it," Suzy said with a dramatic sigh. "Okay, catch ya later—and don't do anything I wouldn't do with Hot Buns."

No matter what the differences between them, Suzy was a breath of fresh air in Claire's otherwise dull daytime routine. She laughed under her breath and thought to herself, *If Suzy had any idea what I was doing last night she would probably die of a heart attack on the spot.* She hoped that would be over before anyone ever knew the lengths she was forced to go through to pay her mother's medical bills. She gathered up her own tray and headed to the front to drop it off.

"How're you doing today, my love?" George asked. George had been with Danvers running the cafeteria for thirty years, hired back in the day Marshall Danvers, Jason's father, started the company. George always had a smile for everyone and, in truth, a soft spot for Claire.

"I'm good, George. Thanks for asking."

"When are you going to let me take you away from all this?"

"Now, what in the world would Sara say, George?" Sara was George's lady friend, as he called her, and the two were just a perfect match.

"Sara would understand if I had to trade up. We got an understanding."

"George, you wouldn't even know how to get up in the morning without Sara. You better hold on to her with both hands. She's a keeper."

"That's true, but a guy can dream, right?"

"You're hopeless, George. You have a good day."

"You too, love. See you tomorrow."

Claire walked down the hall to the elevator bank. No corners were cut with the decor of Danvers International. Everything here was gleaming: white marble floors, soft off-white walls, and stainless steel elevators with mahogany walls inside. As she stepped into the elevator she once again forced herself to remain calm. Confronting her fear of enclosed spaces was what forced her to take the elevator every day instead of the stairs. While the stairs might be better for her physically, conquering her claustrophobia was far more important.

Danvers International was a huge glass-and-steel building with twenty-five floors. Jason Danvers' office was on the twenty-third floor, and his personal space was on the twenty-fourth and twenty-fifth floors. The door to Jason's large office was closed, as usual. Putting away her purse in the bottom drawer of her desk, she settled into her chair in the reception area.

Jason liked the office to be very impersonal and she was always careful to have no personal items on her desk. His one concession to some type of informality was to address her by her first name, and he liked to be addressed by his as well.

She had been working as Jason's assistant for three years. Her job generally required her to handle all the liaising with clients, suppliers, and other staff. She was Jason's right hand and ensured that all appointments, meetings, and projects were scheduled and staffed as needed. Her office life was never slow or boring. He was a fair boss and always treated her well. In the time they had worked together they had managed to create a comfortable relationship. It wasn't exactly a friendship, because they didn't have personal conversations. It was more of a mutual respect for each other's abilities.

She was checking her e-mail when the office door opened and he strolled out. His normally wavy brown hair was rumpled as if he had been running his hands through it, and his mouth was pulled in a tight line.

"Claire, could I have a word with you in my office?"

Normally he just relied on the telephone to give orders, so it was somewhat of a surprise to be summoned personally. He waited for her to step out from behind her desk and precede him into his office. Claire was initially surprised at how at odds Jason's office seemed to be with his personality. Jason was very direct and a person of few words. His clothing favored darker colors with his style usually expensive and conservative. At thirty-five years old, he could easily pass for someone in his twenties. His office, however, had a nautical motif. Jason had several beautiful colorful pictures of the ocean and various beach scenes, and the room was reminiscent of an expensive seaside hotel.

She had been shocked the first time she'd entered his office at how comfortable and soothing it was compared to the rest of Danvers International. She'd heard from various employees that Jason loved the sea, which was a major reason Danvers International headquarters remained in Myrtle Beach, South Carolina, rather than moving to bigger cities that would offer more benefits to a company of its size.

She'd spent a lot of time in this office imagining rolling around on the floor buck naked with her boss—carpet burns be damned! Just because Suzy was her best friend didn't mean she had to tell her that her fantasies of Jason were probably better than anything Suzy had dared to imagine. Carefully schooling her face into a neutral expression, she looked at Jason with what she hoped would pass for professionalism and not "do me" desperation.

"Claire, I need you to work this weekend. I know I usually don't impose a weekend work schedule; however, the contracts for Mericom are supposed to be finished on Saturday, and I'll need you to be on hand to handle any last-minute changes that may take place."

"That's not a problem. What time should I be in the office on Saturday?"

"That's the problem. Unfortunately I'll be going out of town this evening to Columbia, and I'll need you to travel with me. My friend Harold is getting married on Sunday, and I'm expected at his home for the weekend since I'm in the wedding party."

Oh, great. I've not worked weekends for over a year and rarely travel on business and now I'm being asked to do both!

"Jason, I have a previous family engagement for the weekend, but I'll be glad to be in the office during the day on both Saturday and Sunday."

"I'm afraid that isn't going to work. I don't need to remind you how big this deal with Mericom is to Danvers, do I?"

He had been working for close to a year on the acquisition of Mericom. Danvers International was the second biggest communications company in the U.S., and with the addition of Mericom, Danvers would move firmly into first place.

"No, that's fine. Would it be a problem if you gave me directions so that I could meet you tomorrow morning?"

"I guess that's okay. I'll e-mail the information to you shortly."

When Jason's cell phone rang, she took the opportunity to excuse herself from his office. *Crap, crap, crap, what am I going to do about this weekend?!*

Chapter Two

Claire pulled out her cell phone and walked down the hall to the ladies' restroom. She looked under the stalls to make sure she was alone and called her friend Pam. *Geez, has my life become a sneak-to-the-bathroom kind of covert operation? Am I back to being fifteen again?*

"Hello, you have reached the voicemail of Pam Stalls at Partiez Plus. Please leave a message after the tone, and I'll return your call as soon as possible."

She rolled her eyes as her call went straight to voicemail. "Pam, it's Claire. I have a problem with Saturday night. My boss needs me to work this weekend. I have to travel to Columbia, and I won't be able to work the Hunter party. I'm sorry about leaving you hanging at the last minute." She closed her cell phone and leaned her forehead against the bathroom wall and tried not to focus on what kind of nasty things had been there before her.

She first began working weekends for Pam quite by

chance. With her mother's medical bills piling up, she had gotten desperate for a second income to help make a dent in the constant stream of expenses. While pondering how successful someone such as herself might be as a hooker, an ad in the Sunday paper caught her attention. *Okay, so it's Sunday, and I shouldn't have been wondering if I could sell my body for extra money while skipping church. Talk about guilt!*

Partiez Plus, a party-planning company, was advertising a flexible evening and weekend schedule. Perfect! She'd called that day and talked to Pam, who was frantically trying to find an assistant for a local celebrity's big party that evening. When Claire had inquired about the job opening, Pam had said if she could start in two hours, then she was hired. That had been the beginning of a quick friendship and some very busy weekends.

Partiez Plus covered everything from children's birthday parties to adult bachelor and bachelorette parties. Although very hesitant to work the bachelor parties at first, Claire had been doing them now almost exclusively for a year. If someone had told her a few years ago that she would be jumping out of birthday or bachelor-party cakes, she would have told them they were crazy. But after a while it became just like any other job. Maybe in some small way it gave her a thrill knowing her father would have been horrified that his daughter was doing such a thing.

The bachelor parties paid the best and, with every cent being crucial, she was too hard-pressed for money to stick with the lower-paying parties. The Hunter bachelor party was for a groom-to-be who lived in Florence, which was around two hours from Myrtle Beach. She regularly traveled on the weekends when working the parties. This party paid very well and she felt sick to be forced to miss it even though Jason was generously paying overtime.

Just as she was leaving the bathroom, her cell phone rang. She saw Pam's name on the caller ID and answered the phone saying, "Pam, I'm really sorry about this."

"Claire, I've got to have you this weekend. You know that I can't get anyone else on this short notice, and these people are VIPs and use our services for a lot of different functions. If I'm forced to cancel, I'll lose their future business."

"Pam, I don't know what to say. I can't get out of it. I have to travel to Columbia in the morning and will be there through Sunday."

"Columbia, hmmm," muttered Pam. "That's only an hour from Florence, which is closer to the party than you are now. Do you think you could get away for a while on Saturday evening, do the party, and then return to Columbia?"

A small flicker of hope sprang to life within her. "Pam, I don't know."

"I'll double your rate if you can, Claire. I'm desperate."

"Let me ask Jason if he'll need me in the evening, and I'll let you know." After bribes and pleading from Pam, she closed the phone and headed back toward her office. She returned to her desk and tried to work up the nerve to ask Jason about Saturday night. The switchboard showed that he was on the telephone. *Okay, chicken, go ahead and e-mail him instead of asking him in person.* She opened her e-mail program and wrote Jason a short line inquiring about Saturday night and just stopped herself from signing it *Love or Lust, Claire.* A few moments later the door to Jason's office opened, and he stepped out with his briefcase.

"Did you get the directions I sent you?"

"Yes, I have them."

As he was leaving he said, "About Saturday night—if you'd like some time off, that's fine. I'll also be going out to dinner with Harold and some other friends."

"Oh, that's great. I have some family close to the area that I would really like to visit." *Liar, liar, pants on fire.*

"See you tomorrow," Jason replied as he shut the door.

Holy moly, Suzy is right. That man does have a smoking-hot set of buns—whew! Breathing a sigh of relief, she started clearing off her desk and shutting her computer down. Bringing out her cell phone, she sent a text to

Pam to let her know that she would be available to do the party on Saturday evening as planned. She gave her watch a quick glance and hurriedly gathered her purse. Her mother and Louise would be waiting on her for dinner.

Chapter Three

Claire's mother had been diagnosed with Type 1 diabetes almost five years ago, and despite their best efforts, each year seemed to take a further toll on her health. To add to the problem, her mother was also in the early stages of Alzheimer's. Louise had been her mother and father's housekeeper for as long as Claire could remember. Her father had been a corporate lawyer and prided himself on leading a certain lifestyle. Being waited on and able to brag about having a maid had been part of that lifestyle. When Claire's father and sister were killed in a tragic auto accident three years earlier, Louise had moved in with her mother to provide some much-needed companionship.

Her mother had never really recovered from the shock and blamed herself for the accident. Her father was always very particular about their meals. When her mother didn't purchase what he wanted for dinner, Claire's father had insisted on going to the supermarket to get the correct items, since no one else was intelligent enough to make sure it was handled correctly. Her father had also discovered that day that her sister had been seeing a boy whom he deemed unacceptable, so he had made her go along so he could spend the travel time lecturing her. In a sense, her father and sister died for his wanting gratin potatoes rather than plain mashed potatoes.

Since the fast decline of her mother's health, Louise had become an absolute necessity. Claire didn't know what she would do without her. As her mother's memory steadily worsened, Louise ensured that her blood sugar was checked regularly and that her medication was given at the correct times. Claire had worked out an agreement with Louise to provide her with a room and a small salary. Even though Louise's salary was modest, it was still a struggle to meet most months, with the price of her mother's medication and the upkeep on the house.

She locked the door to her office and walked to the elevator, taking a deep breath to avoid the suffocating feeling of the confined space as she waited for the doors to open. It was past six on a Friday evening and most of the office had already left for the day. She waited for the elevator door to open to the parking garage, which was another source of discomfort for her. Would she ever get over this claustrophobia she'd been cursed with her whole life?

Claire opened the door to her Toyota compact and slid onto the threadbare seat. Affording a new car in the future seemed very out of reach. Luckily, Daisy, as she called her car, seemed to be dependable and loyal. But she was by no stretch of the imagination a man magnet, unless he was a repairman.

She turned onto the street toward her mother's home. Her mother lived a few miles from the beach in Murrells Inlet. Although close enough to Myrtle Beach to be very busy during the summer tourist season, Murrells Inlet still had a certain small-town charm. As she turned in the driveway of the two-story home, she stopped to appreciate the exterior. For those looking for the fairy tale of a house with a white picket fence, this was it. It was only when you looked closer that the last few years of neglect were starting to show. And life had been nothing like a fairy tale for the people who had lived in the house.

Her father had been an overbearing, manipulative man who verbally abused the family while he was alive. Nothing was ever good enough to please him. If her sister, Chrissie, or she didn't make all *A*s in school, they were stupid and lazy; if they did, it was because they took easy courses that anyone could pass. Everyone walked on eggshells around him, terrified of what would set him off that day.

Claire, desperate to escape, had planned to move out once she started college. Chrissie had begged her to stay at least until she graduated, terrified of being left to face their father's wrath alone. She tried to shield Chrissie as much as she could, making herself the prime target for her father. He had never physically struck them, nor did she think he had her mother. Words were his weapon of choice and he used them like knives.

Studying the house, Claire thought again how much easier it would be if her mother lived in a condominium that included maintenance and upkeep, because the price of maintaining her home as well as her medication was staggering. She would also love never to have to see this house again. After the death of her father, her mother had lived comfortably on his life insurance payment for a few years. But in the last year that money had dwindled, and now Claire was forced to pick up the medical bills that Medicare didn't cover, which seemed to be numerous, as well as the maintenance of the home. With a sigh, she made her way up the front walk and was met at the door by Louise. No matter how bad her day, Louise always made her smile. Claire's five-feet-seven frame seemed to tower over Louise, who stood just five feet tall.

Louise still insisted on getting a curly perm in her hair every few months, and also claimed that as long as they made hair color, she would never be gray. She might not be gray, but Claire had seen various other shades over the years when the hair color went wrong. At the present, it was more of a dark brown with what could possibly be burgundy highlights. She gave Louise a hug and entered the foyer of the house. The original hardwood floors caught the light and gleamed. The staircase was straight in front of the door with the dining room to the right and the living room to the left.

"How is Mom doing today, Louise? Did she take all her medications without too much of a fight?"

"She's been having an off day but seems better now." Her mother seemed to be having many off days lately. "Her blood sugar was low this morning," continued Louise. "And that really takes her a while to recover from."

At that moment, Claire's mother walked in from the kitchen at the back of the house, and her eyes just seemed to light up. Her mother rushed forward and grabbed her in a hug, excitedly saying, "Chrissie, I knew you'd come by today. I've been waiting for you!"

Claire looked over at Louise and saw the tears in the corners of her eyes. Louise stepped forward and put her arm around her mother and said, "Now, Evelyn, you know this isn't Chrissie. This is Claire, remember?"

Her mother looked at Claire in confusion and Claire could see the agitation beginning. "I think I know who my own daughter is," her mother said indignantly.

Saddened, Claire looked at Louise and said, "It doesn't matter, Louise."

The confusion and the agitation that followed were the reasons Claire was forced to have a separate residence even though it would have been much easier financially for them to live together. For some reason, her mother never seemed to forget Louise, but she often confused Claire with Chrissie or didn't recognize her at all. Even though she forgot that Chrissie was dead at times, she never asked after her husband. It was as if she could accept his death but couldn't process Chrissie's.

"I have dinner ready," Louise said. She gently turned her mother around and they all headed toward the kitchen. With just her mother, Louise, and herself, the formal dining room had long ago stopped being used in favor of the smaller breakfast nook in the kitchen. Louise made a simple dinner of tomato bisque and ham and cheese sandwiches. Louise settled her mother in a chair, and Claire took a seat on the other side of the table, careful to keep from startling her mother in her present state of mind.

Her mother suddenly looked at her and said in an excited voice, "Oh, Claire, you made it for dinner! When did you come in, honey?"

"I got here a few moments ago, Mom." With a sad expression on her face, Louise looked over at Claire as she sat down.

"How was your day, honey?" her mother asked.

"It was fine, Mom, just busy as usual. I'm going to Columbia on business this weekend, so I won't see you again until Sunday evening."

"Oh, Claire, you work so hard. Doesn't she, Louise?"

Louise winked at her. "You know these young people today, Evelyn—work, work, work."

The rest of the meal was spent in relaxed conversation. After dinner was finished Louise led Claire's mother into the living room and settled her in front of the TV to watch her favorite soap opera on DVR. When she returned to the kitchen she looked at Claire and said, "The roof is leaking again in the master bedroom upstairs."

Looking at Louise in dismay, she said, "I just had that fixed last winter. How in the world is it leaking again?"

"Honey, it was two years ago, and that's about how long the roofer said it would hold."

She sat down in a kitchen chair and wearily closed her eyes for a moment.

"The Lord never gives us more than we can handle. Things will turn around soon—just have faith," Louise soothed.

"Faith has been in real short supply lately. I'm not sure how much longer I can handle the upkeep on this house, Louise. I know it would just kill Mom to have to move."

"Honey, we will do what we need to do. Your mother would be confused, but I think she would adjust in time. Let me call my nephew, Brent. He's a good handyman and might be cheaper than a roofing company."

"Thanks. I don't know what I would do without you," Claire said as she stood up and walked across the kitchen to hug her. "I'll call you this weekend while I'm in Columbia, but if anything at all comes up, call me, Louise, and I'll come straight back home."

"You don't worry about us. We will be just fine."

Claire walked into the living room and said, "Mom, I'm leaving now." Claire leaned down to give her mother a kiss.

Her mother absently patted her cheek and said, "Okay, Chrissie, I'll see you tomorrow," and went back to her soap opera. Not bothering to correct her, she called out one last good-bye to Louise and made her way out the door to where Daisy patiently waited. She backed out of the driveway and headed to the south side of Myrtle Beach and her small one-bedroom apartment.

Chapter Four

Myrtle Beach was a busy tourist town, and rent was not cheap. Claire had been fortunate to find a reasonably priced apartment in a quieter area of town that was a little further away from the ocean than most of the tourist crowd liked to be. She spotted her neighbor William—"but call me Billy"—in the parking lot and desperately looked for another spot. The lot was completely full except for her space in front of her apartment, so it was either flee or suck it up and park. She could see Billy's eyes zero in on her as she pulled into her spot.

Billy was on the short side, with a pudgy build and hair that looked as if he poured oil straight on it each day to slick it down. He had a very disturbing habit of adjusting himself constantly. She could only hope this was a bad habit and not an indication of how much she excited him. She shuddered at the last thought as he strolled toward her in his nauseating trying-to-be-sexy way. She hurriedly stepped from her car and attempted to walk toward her apartment door.

"Hey, good looking, long time, no see," began Billy.

"Er . . . yeah, long time. I'm in a bit of a hurry, though."

Completely ignoring that last line, he continued. "I've been trying to catch you at home. I got two tickets to a Neil Diamond show. This tribute band is so good you'd never know the difference."

"That sounds, um . . . lovely, but I'll be going out of town for a while on business and have no idea when I'll be back."

"That's okay. It's not until next month, and you should be back by then, right?"

"It could be a really long trip," she stressed. "I'll have to get back to you."

She cringed as he leaned in closer. "Just give us a chance, Claire. Old Billy will rock your world." Another annoying problem: Billy liked to talk about himself in the third person.

Thanks to either good timing or what she liked to think of as divine intervention, the neighbor two doors down came out of his apartment and yelled, "Hey, Billy, I need a lift to the store, man." She took that as her cue to run like hell and took off toward her apartment. She quickly unlocked her door and almost fell inside in her haste.

She went straight to the couch and lay down, intending to take a short rest before packing for the trip. She shuddered one more time at being cornered by William "but call me Billy" and hoped she never got that desperate. It had been more than three years now since she'd actually had sex. Three long years and to say that she was so horny she literally followed the hunky mailman around like a stalker was an understatement. *But please, Lord, never let me get that desperate. Maybe it is time for one of those vibrating rabbits Suzy has been suggesting.*

When she opened her eyes again, dawn was just starting to break. She jumped up from the couch, her heart pounding. She'd slept through the night, and it was now seven o'clock. She ran into her bedroom and grabbed a suitcase out of the closet, dropping it onto the bed. She began pulling slacks and shirts out, and within an hour she was fully packed and ready to leave for Columbia. She said a quick prayer to herself that she actually had some clothes that would match as she locked her door and packed the suitcase in her car.

A few hours later, she was on I-20 heading toward Columbia. She vowed to stop at the next rest area to look over her directions from Jason. She finally allowed herself to take a deep breath and relax. She would probably be a bit later than Jason intended but hopefully there would be no news of the contracts yet and she would have a moment to get settled in. She turned on her radio and heard Jon Bon Jovi proudly belting out "Livin' on a Prayer."

When she saw the sign for a rest area, she pulled in and went over her directions. After a quick restroom visit, she was back on the road, and traffic was picking up as she drew closer to the city of Columbia. She spotted her exit up ahead, took it, and turned onto the adjoining road. Thanks to Jason's very precise directions, she was soon turning into the driveway of Jason's friend Harold.

Jason had told her that Harold's family ran a large ranch that bred and sold expensive racehorses internationally. The buildings and stables close to the house seemed to be a hub of activity. She felt like she was looking back at an episode of her mother's old favorite nighttime soap opera, *Dallas*. You almost expected to see Bobby or J. R. Ewing walking out the door. Maybe she could be Pam for the weekend, and Jason could be Bobby. She chuckled to herself at that thought as she pulled her car into an available parking space. She spared a glance at her reflection in the rearview mirror and opened the door to exit the car.

She lifted out her small suitcase from the trunk just as an enormous dog bounded up. Reflexes kicking in, she quickly jumped back as the dog skidded to a stop and proceeded to lick her hand.

"Wolf, you crazy dog, stop!" She looked up as a pretty girl with a rather harassed air approached the car. "I'm sorry about the impromptu bath, but Wolf has never met a stranger he didn't lick. I'm Elizabeth, Harold's fiancée, and you have already met Harold's mutt, Wolf."

Claire gave Wolf a quick pat and scratch behind the ears. She offered her other hand to Elizabeth. "Hi, I'm Claire, Jason's assistant."

"Good to meet you, Claire. Harold asked me to keep an eye out for you since he and Jason have gone riding and have not yet returned."

"This is a beautiful place. I had no idea that this was such a large ranch."

"Harold's family has been in the business for generations. His parents retired to Florida a few years ago and now Harold is running the business—or, actually, it seems to be running us most days, but we love it. Come on inside. I made up a guest room upstairs for you near Jason's room. How long have you worked with him?"

She followed Elizabeth into a surprisingly homey entryway and replied, "For almost three years." Suddenly, something under her foot made a loud squeaking sound. Automatically jumping back with an apology forming on her lips, she looked down to see a plastic bone that she'd overlooked on her way across the foyer. She looked over at Elizabeth and they both burst out laughing.

"As you can see, Claire, we've a pretty informal home, and Wolf is generally the boss of it."

She was pleasantly surprised at how friendly Elizabeth was and how comfortable she felt with her.

"Jason, Harold, and I all went to college together," continued Elizabeth. "And I just think the world of Jason. The other groomsmen are staying at a hotel closer to downtown and they're all going out tonight for what I highly suspect is a bachelor party for Harold." Elizabeth laughed. "Harold is on the shy side, and the guys love to embarrass him. I think Jason and Harold were always close because, with Harold being the quiet one and Jason being the serious one, they seemed to blend well together. That's the reason Jason is staying here with us and the others are staying at a hotel. Harold was afraid they'd do something to embarrass him in front of the neighbors."

She followed Elizabeth up the stairs to the end of the hall. Elizabeth opened a door, saying, "This is your room." Pointing to another door, she indicated an adjoining bathroom. "The door on the left side opens into a connecting bedroom and Jason will be there. Jason has an office set up in the sitting area of his room, and I thought it would be easier for you to work together if you were close."

"Thanks so much, Elizabeth. I really appreciate everything."

"Oh, call me Liz. Everyone else does. I'll leave you to settle in. If you need anything I'll be working at the other end of the hall in the office on the right, so feel free to drop in. I expect the guys to be back around lunchtime, and we can all have a bite on the patio outside."

"Thanks again, Liz." After a few moments, Claire heard the door open down the hall as Liz went into her office. Her room held a queen-sized bed in the center with a lovely pale yellow comforter that matched the soothing color of the walls. An antique chest sat at the foot of the bed with a dresser of similar design directly in front of it against the wall. She opened a door beside the bathroom and found the closet to be empty. She quickly unpacked and hung her clothing up to avoid them wrinkling further. A quick check of her watch showed it was close to noon, and she wondered what time the men would return for lunch. She took her vanity bag into the bathroom to freshen up and gave an appreciative sigh.

The bathroom had obviously been upgraded recently and contained a huge separate glass-enclosed shower and a lovely Jacuzzi bathtub. The floors were white marble, and the walls were the same yellow color of the bedroom. She used one of the washcloths that had been laid out on the vanity to wash her face and reapplied a light tinted moisturizer along with pale pink lipstick. She released her hair from its clip and attempted to tame it into something tolerable before she put it back up.

She accidentally knocked over her vanity bag, and the contents scattered all over the floor. She smothered a curse under her breath as she leaned over to pick up the mess and promptly hit her head on the corner of the vanity. *Ouch!* She stood with her hand over the injured area and saw in the mirror that she'd somehow managed to make a small cut. *Damn, why must I always be such a klutz?* "Mishaps," as she termed them, had plagued her for most of her life. She went back into the bedroom to retrieve her purse, which held the emergency box of Band-Aids she never left home without. Suddenly the door at the opposite end of the room opened, and Jason stepped through.

"Claire, I heard a crash. I knocked a couple of times but there was no answer." She froze as Jason walked into the room. Looking incredible in a pair of well-worn jeans that hugged him in all the right places and a black polo shirt, he was staring at her with a look of impatience on his handsome face. The room that had seemed very large at first now seemed to shrink to an almost suffocating size with Jason in it.

Taken by surprise at his sudden appearance, she stuttered, "I—I hit my head and was looking for a Band-Aid."

"Good Lord, you have blood on your hand. Let me see your head."

"No, that's okay, Jason. Give me a minute, and I'll take care of it."

"For God's sake, Claire, give me the damn thing." Too startled by his outburst to do anything else, she didn't resist as he removed the Band-Aid from her hand and motioned at her to go ahead of him into the bathroom. Despite the impatience in his words, his hands were gentle as he moved her hand aside and surveyed the cut. "How in the world did you manage this?"

"I dropped my bag on the floor and was leaning down to pick it up when I accidentally hit the vanity corner."

"It's already starting to swell and will probably cause a bruise." He wet another cloth and gently dabbed at the corner of the cut. Then he removed the Band-Aid from the package, expertly applying it to her head. "That probably needs antibiotic cream. I'll ask Liz for some at lunch. Do you feel okay? We can also ask Liz for some painkillers if it's hurting at all."

"No, really, it's fine. You didn't need to bother. I'm used to patching myself up from my mishaps."

"Does this kind of thing happen a lot?"

"I seem to be quite a magnet for random household accidents. After a while you learn to patch yourself up quickly," she said with a laugh.

Claire gave him an uncertain smile as he suddenly paused, his blue eyes seeming to fixate on her for a moment. As if noticing her confusion, he flushed and turned his head away mumbling, "I don't think I've ever noticed how, uh . . . pretty your hair is. Why do you always wear it up?"

Self-consciously patting her hair down in an effort to tame it, she said, "It's rather hard to control, so it's easier to keep it up."

"That's a real shame," he said so quietly she wasn't even sure if she'd heard him correctly.

He bent over and started to pick up the contents of her makeup bag from the floor. She couldn't help but admire his long, lean form. Those jeans did things for his butt that should be against the law. She had to fight the urge to slide her hand right down that hot set of buns and give them a squeeze. Suzy would be hyperventilating if she were here to witness this. She looked away before she was caught ogling the boss's butt. She had to stifle a giggle as she imagined the horrified expression on his face if, as his assistant, she suddenly gave in to the urge to feel him up.

He put the bag on the counter and then put the washcloth he used in the hamper. He walked back out to the bedroom toward the adjoining door, then looked over his shoulder and said, "Meet me in the hall in five minutes. We'll go down for lunch and then work for a few hours this afternoon."

As the door shut behind him, she took a deep breath and slowly released it. She quickly returned to the bathroom and put her hair in its usual boring ponytail and sighed. *Maybe Suzy is right—it is time for a makeover.* How many times could someone wear brown, beige, or tan and not turn into a sofa cover eventually?

She headed to the door and found Jason waiting in the hall for her. She noticed him looking at her hair, and she hoped a stray piece wasn't sticking up. He said, "You should always wear your hair down. You look like a different person."

Startled, because he never made comments of a personal nature, she could feel her cheeks starting to burn. Another misfortune as far as she was concerned was not only that she was prone to a lot of mishaps, but she also still blushed like a teenager.

She quickly looked away from his intense gaze, feeling like she'd somehow let him down by putting her hair up. "I'm not sure where the patio is located, so lead the way." Thankfully he took the hint and turned and headed down the hall to the stairway.

They walked through a comfortable-looking living area and then through an ultra-modern kitchen. She caught a glimpse of Liz and Harold sitting at a large wrought-iron table through glass patio doors. Jason opened the door and stood back to allow her to walk out ahead of him. After the dim light of the house it took several moments for her eyes to adjust to the glare of the bright sun. Standing up from the table, Harold approached her and in a quiet voice said, "Claire, I'm Harold. I'm so pleased to meet you."

Harold was tall and thin with sandy blond hair that was beginning to thin on the top. She could imagine that he had probably been all legs when he was growing up. A pair of gold-rimmed glasses framed green eyes that could easily have been his best feature.

She took the offered hand and said, "It's a pleasure, Harold. I really appreciate your hospitality."

"No problem at all. I know that you and Jason have work to do this weekend, but I also hope you will have time to look around the ranch, and maybe we can all go for a horseback ride tomorrow morning before you leave."

Jason pulled a seat out for her at the table beside Liz and replied wryly, "I don't know about that, Harold. Claire has a bit of a problem with mishaps, so it might be healthier for her to remain on her own two feet."

Claire could feel the curious gazes of Harold and Liz as Jason took the seat on her other side. Liz reached over to pat her shoulder and said, "I'm sure we can find something you'd enjoy doing while you're here. If you'd rather not ride, maybe you could take a nice walk around the ranch with Wolf. It's really beautiful this time of the year."

"I'm sure you will both be too busy tomorrow with the wedding for anything else, but thank you very much for the offer."

She felt the urge to kick Jason under the table for his previous comment. She settled for shooting him a dirty look, and received a knowing smirk in return.

"I hope you like chili, Claire. It's one of the few dishes that I can actually make," Liz said and laughed. "We have some fresh fruit for dessert."

"Chili sounds great, Liz." She took a bite of the fragrant chili and looked around the ranch. In the distance, she could see a huge building with a corral in the front; within it, several men led horses. Harold explained that those horses were being trained for specific buyers. One buyer was purchasing a horse for his daughter, who had been an avid rider but was tragically blinded in an accident last year. The daughter wanted to continue to ride, and they were working on a method of horse training for the disabled. Liz enthusiastically picked up the conversation as Harold paused for a moment to enjoy his lunch.

"This is a project that Harold and I started last year, and it's become so successful. Training horses for a person with a specific handicap is challenging and often a long process. But when we saw the tears of the first young lady we trained a horse for—she lost a leg in an auto accident—we both knew this was our calling. Harold's parents mainly dealt in raising cattle. Training and selling race horses was really a hobby for them. This new area is our labor of love and, although it has taken an enormous amount of time and training, we feel so blessed to be able to give people back their dreams."

"Wow, that's amazing. You must both be so proud of what you're doing."

Jason laughed. "Harold and Liz may be the only truly selfless people I've ever met, and to prove that point, look at that mongrel of theirs that they lavish all their love on." She looked in the direction Jason was pointing and saw Wolf running around in a circle chasing his tail, finally falling over as though the effort had cost him greatly. Everyone laughed, and the meal continued in companionable conversation about the local area and stories of other horses they'd trained.

She was surprised to find this to be the most enjoyable meal she'd shared with anyone in a long time. Most of her meals with her mother and Louise were spent in constant trepidation of her mother becoming agitated when her memory lapsed. Meals with Suzy seemed to revolve around Claire getting out more and getting a social life or, at the very least, just getting laid. So this lunch seemed remarkably pressure free. Even Jason, who normally was so intense to be around, appeared to be relaxed as he pointed out areas of interest around the ranch or told stories from his and Harold's college days. It was nice to feel like a part of their group, and even though she was Jason's secretary and there in an official capacity, she still felt relaxed and carefree, a rare sensation for her.

Claire insisted on helping Liz clear the table. They walked in the kitchen and loaded the dishwasher together. "I know this is none of my business—and Harold says that never stops me—but how long have you and Jason been seeing each other?" asked Liz.

Completely confused by the question, she looked at Liz and asked, "Do you mean how long have I been working for him?"

"No, how long have you been dating him?" This struck Claire as hysterical and she began to laugh.

When she could finally catch her breath, she looked at Liz and said between peals of laughter, "He would probably be surprised to realize I'm female, much less the object of his romantic interests!"

Liz joined in her laughter and said, "Oh, I think he knows you're female, all right, from the vibes I was getting across the table. I think there was more than the chili steaming over there."

"Trust me—he'd have more romantic vibes toward Wolf than toward me. We have a strictly professional relationship." She was vastly amused to think of how shocked Jason would be that Liz thought he had feelings for her. His first question would probably be "Claire who?" and the second would be "Are you kidding?"

At just that moment, the object of their laughter strolled into the kitchen and, God help her, she had to admit he looked better than any man had a right to. Why must she always feel like she was in perpetual heat around this man? She'd actually been around other hot guys before and hadn't felt like her underwear was on fire, so what was the problem here?

"Claire, are you ready to work for a few hours before we have to break for the evening?"

"Yes, that's fine. I'm ready if you are." *Oh, yeah, baby, I'm more than ready. . . .* She shared one last secret smile with Liz before once again letting Jason lead her as they went back upstairs.

Chapter Five

Jason's room repeated the same comfortable theme as Claire's room. The walls were painted a pale blue color; there was a matching comforter on the queen-sized bed and another chest at the foot of the bed. "I love the antique touches that Liz and Harold have in their home," she said appreciably as she pointed to the chest.

"Collecting antiques is a hobby they have, and when Liz finds a bargain on a rare piece Harold says she's in sheer bliss for days," replied Jason with an affectionate smile. She couldn't help but think of how nice it would be to be the object of that affection. She quickly looked away from Jason and walked toward the desk he had set up in the sitting area.

"Claire, I've forwarded the first draft of the contract to your e-mail. I have the printer ready to connect to the laptop computer for you to work on." She started to go under the table to retrieve the printer plug when Jason said, "No, let me do that!" She jumped in surprise, banging her head on the underside of the table with the cord clutched in her hand. She winced in pain, reaching up to rub her head. She crawled from under the table and sat back on her heels while she felt her latest head injury.

"Damn, Claire, I'm sorry! I shouldn't have startled you like that. Are you okay?" Jason gently removed her hand and ran his own over the area she'd been holding. "I don't see any blood this time, but you're probably going to have yet another bump. You really weren't kidding about the mishaps, were you? I have to take the blame for this one, though, since I scared you."

He extended a hand to help her to her feet. He then took the cord from her and plugged it into the computer. He led her gently to a chair and said in an amused tone, "Let's keep you away from all sharp objects, and for God's sake, please don't go near the scissors." She laughed and marveled at how relaxed she felt around him for the first time since she'd started working for him. He seemed to be a different person away from the office, and unfortunately, despite her best efforts, she found *this* Jason far too attractive for her own good. She tried not to dwell on that disturbing fact as she powered on her computer.

She took a quick glance at her watch and saw that it was now almost two thirty. She would need to be on the road by five to allow time to travel to the bachelor party this evening. She said a quick prayer that they were finished with work in time for her to get ready.

"Claire, I'll need you to start making the changes

that I've listed on the notebook on the desk. The first change will go in paragraph one." He leaned over her shoulder and started pointing out the area in which to make the change, and she caught the fragrance of his cologne. Distracted by just how good the musky scent smelled on him, she really hoped that she didn't look like a complete idiot when he started asking her for suggestions on the wording of the phrase he wished to insert. *What's wrong with me today? I've worked for the man for three years, and I'm now suddenly a constantly drooling idiot like the other women at work! Maybe Suzy is right—I do need to get a life!*

"Claire, did you hear me?" Giving a guilty start, she asked him to repeat his question in hopes that he would not think she was a complete incompetent. She went to work on the first draft while Jason took a chair on the other side of the desk and started booting up his computer. She couldn't help but notice the way the sunlight made his hair shine, and she also saw red highlights that she'd never noticed before. She quickly looked away before he caught her staring at him. She lost herself in the revision and was startled when Jason looked up and said, "We should probably call it a day. It's close to five, and I need to get ready. I believe you also have plans for the evening?"

She looked at her watch, surprised to see that so much time had already passed. "I've got most of the revisions complete if you'd like to look over them before I close the program."

"No, that's okay; we will go over everything in the morning, so go ahead and close up for the evening."

She gathered her papers in a neat stack and noticed how stiff her back was as she stood. Without thinking she took a long, leisurely stretch and looked up to find Jason watching her intently. Her face flushed and she looked away from his gaze, saying, "If you don't need anything else, I'm going to change and get going."

He cleared his throat and said, "Um, no problem. Have a good evening."

She quickly walked through the adjoining door, quietly clicking the lock into place behind her. She would rather have him find her unconscious than walk in unannounced after another mishap. In the bathroom she looked longingly at the bathtub, but knew that it was a luxury she didn't have time for. She settled instead for the shower, letting it warm up as she undressed. She gave a murmur of bliss as the hot water cascaded over her tired shoulders, wincing when the water hit the new bump on her head. She gently worked some shampoo through her hair and enjoyed the feel of the water soothing away the fatigue of the day. Loath to cut the shower short, she finished up quickly, knowing that she was pressed for time.

She wrapped a towel around her hair and shrugged on the ratty old pink bathrobe that she'd thought to bring along. She plugged in her small dryer and started the task of drying her hair. She knew she should really get it cut in a shorter style to reduce some of the drying time, but she considered it her one item of vanity even though she wore it up more than down.

When she'd first started training to work the bachelor parties, Pam immediately removed the clip from her hair and told her that men loved seeing long hair. This statement really gave her pause as she'd understood from Pam that the clients for these parties were strictly upper class and instead of expecting a stripper performance at a bachelor party, they were content with a pretty girl in a corset and garter belt; no articles of clothing removed.

When Pam explained the show's wardrobe, Claire originally turned her down flat out. She'd never worn less than a one-piece swimsuit in public, and she certainly didn't intend to lose her inhibitions in front of a room full of strangers. The following day, she had received the news that her mother's furnace needed to be replaced. There was no way she could afford the new furnace *and* her mother's medicine; thus she ended up with a second job that she never would have imagined doing in a lifetime.

The theme for most bachelor parties offered by Partiez Plus was what she imagined a country club for wealthy golfers would offer, with expensive furniture, including luxurious wingback chairs and mahogany tables arranged into several intimate seating areas. There were crystal decanters on each table offering an array of liquors. A box of imported cigars was available for the more adventurous guests. Waitstaff circulated discreetly, seeing to every need.

A few hours into the evening, a large cake was rolled into the center of the room and the bachelor in question was given a ringside seat—or in this case, a cake-side seat—and the music was cued. At just the right moment, a small spotlight flashed to the cake and—voilà!—out pops a girl with her arms raised in the air! In this case, the girl was Claire. She would then smile and wave to the guest of honor as well as to the others in the bachelor party. After a few moments, she would be assisted down from the cake and would walk up to the bachelor, give him a hug, a bottle of Cristal, and wish him a very happy life.

Generally, she would then exit the area and change into the traditional uniform of the other waitstaff and continue assisting with the party. She couldn't believe she'd gotten so comfortable with these parties that she hardly gave them much thought anymore. The men were indeed generally well behaved, and her moment in the spotlight was short. The tips were very generous and were split among the party staff. Some tips were left specifically for her, but she always insisted that these be divided among everyone as well.

She hurriedly finished drying her hair and went into the bedroom to pull on a tan pair of slacks and a soft purple sweater. She took out the small bag she usually carried to the parties and checked to make sure she had everything she needed, then went back to the bathroom to reapply her makeup. Unfortunately, working the bachelor parties necessitated it be heavier than she would usually wear. The spotlight tended to make her face look pale, and her eyes seemed to disappear. She liberally applied a heavy base to her face along with a pink blush, black eyeliner, and mascara.

Her green eyes were sparkling by the time she finished adding some dark shadow to her eyelids. Even though she didn't like the feel of the makeup, she had to admit that it gave her a somewhat exotic look that she normally lacked. She returned to the other room and gathered her bag and her purse and stepped out into the hall. She looked down to open her purse and locate her car keys while walking toward the stairway. Suddenly the air left her body in a whoosh as she ran into a hard wall. Hands reached out to steady her as she looked up into Jason's amused blue eyes.

"I believe this is your third *mishap* of the day, but who's counting, right?" Jason laughed. He continued to hold on to her arms as though he had suddenly forgotten what he was doing. She was frozen as she watched his intent gaze sweep from the top of her head to pause at her lips and then continue on to her breasts. She pulled herself from his grip, her face starting to flame. He slowly, almost reluctantly, released her. "Is there some special occasion today with your family? You seem really dressed up," asked Jason.

She nervously replied, "Um no, not really. I haven't seen them in a while and wanted to look my best." *Are the words "I'm a complete liar" plastered on my forehead?*

"Well, you should certainly have no problem with

that. You look like you're ready for a date," Jason replied tightly.

Oh yeah, I'm ready for a date with a whole room of horny guys in a few hours. "I, um, no, nothing like that," she replied as she turned away to continue down the hall.

"I'll walk you down," Jason said, falling into step behind her.

As she hurriedly made her way to the stairs, she heard Jason say with amusement, "Claire, let's slow down before mishap number four occurs." She forced herself to slow her pace lest she end up at the bottom of the stairs in a heap. She prayed that she would give Jason nothing further to laugh about today.

Harold and Liz walked out of the family room and stopped in the foyer to wait for them. "Wow, you look great." Liz smiled. "You're more than welcome to join my girls' night this evening, Claire."

"Thank you for offering, Liz. But I have family expecting me."

"Please drop by in the family room if you get home early. My friends are a little loud, but are a really great group of ladies, and I know they'd enjoy your company."

She smiled at Liz warmly and thanked her. She was really surprised at how comfortable she was with Liz and Harold. They seemed the exact opposite of Jason, and she was curious as to how the friendship had continued over all these years. Liz and Harold were the type of people to settle down and promptly have two children who were as well-mannered and lovable as they were.

Jason, however, was the type to spend his whole life driven by the next merger, his eye always on the bottom line. When and if he did marry, she could picture him with a cool blonde who spent most of her time shopping and redesigning their penthouse or country home. Try as she might, she couldn't picture him with children, although she could see that, being an only child, there must be pressure to provide the next Danvers heir. It was suddenly quiet and she realized that Jason had asked her a question.

"I'm sorry; I was just going over the directions to my aunt's home in my head. Can you repeat that please?"

His blue eyes twinkled as if to say, *I know you're lying, but I'll let it pass.* "I asked what area you'll be traveling to. Harold and I could give you a lift and pick you up later tonight if we're going to be near your family."

"N-no, that's okay; my aunt lives off the beaten path, so to speak, and it would be too far out of the way," she stammered.

In his quiet voice, Harold said, "Claire, it would be no problem. We'd be happy to drop you off anywhere you need to go."

Hey, great, could you drop me at the gentlemen's club an hour away? My aunt really likes to party. She could feel herself starting to panic as she said, "That's very thoughtful of you both; however, I promised my aunt that I would take her to dinner and I'll need my own car for that. Thank you, though, for offering."

This appeared to satisfy them both and the topic was dropped. Claire looked down at her watch and announced that her aunt would be waiting for her. After saying good-bye to everyone she walked toward the front door. Jason stepped in front of the door and opened it for her, asking, "What time will you be back this evening?"

Wow, she thought. When had Jason assumed a role as her daddy? "I haven't seen my aunt in quite a while, so I plan to spend several hours with her."

Before Jason could respond, she walked quickly out the door and down the walk way to her car. When she risked a quick look over her shoulder, she saw Jason leaning against his black Mercedes, watching her with an unreadable expression on his handsome face. She quickly climbed into her car and buckled her seat belt while trying to control the urge to speed away.

She took a deep breath and turned her car toward Florence. She was familiar with the area where she was working tonight, so she didn't anticipate any problems with finding the location. She was aghast at her sudden reaction to Jason as not only her boss but very much a man. In the time that she'd worked for him, she had, of course, noticed how handsome he was, especially with Suzy pointing it out numerous times a day. Yes, like everyone else in the company, she had plenty of fantasies about various sexual positions with him, but she never actually saw him as a person.

Her fantasies were the same as she would have for Tom Cruise or George Clooney: lust from afar but business as usual each day. Away from the office and the stress of her life, she was seeing him in a different light. She was suddenly noticing things about him that she shouldn't be, like the way his eyes sparkled when he laughed, the way he obviously loved his friends, and, Lord help her, the way those faded Levi's cupped that gorgeous butt. How many times today had she forced herself to stop staring at him? She practically wiped her mouth a few times to make sure she wasn't drooling. She vowed to return things to their usual professional behavior.

After leaving the city of Columbia, Claire noticed the landscape along the road to Florence was rather sparse. Myrtle Beach seemed like Los Angeles compared to the small towns she was now passing through. She knew she was approaching her exit and mentally prepared herself to enter what she called her Partiez Plus Mode.

Chapter Six

She located the address of the party and parked her car in the employee lot. She looked up with a smile as Julie knocked on her car window. She'd met Julie during her first party, and they'd bonded instantly. Julie was a single mother to a precious four-year-old boy named Kyle, and the extra income from working weekends as a bartender for Partiez Plus allowed her to send Kyle to a great preschool close to their home. She was also attending night school to be a registered nurse.

Occasionally Claire watched Kyle for her in the evenings when Julie's regular sitter was not available. "Hey, Claire, are you ready to get your party on?"

She laughed and said, "You bet. Another day, another cake to jump out of." She lifted her bag from the backseat and walked with Julie to the employees' entrance. The two women waved at the usual crew from Partiez Plus as they walked to the ladies' restroom to change clothes.

Claire opened her bag and removed the corset with

matching panties and garter belt that she would use for her cake routine. She also pulled out the waitstaff uniform she would need afterward from her bag. "Do you think our clothes will be okay left in here?"

"Unless one of the men at the bachelor party decides to go drag, I think we're fine," joked Julie.

She stepped into one of the stalls and began taking off her clothes and putting on the sexy lingerie. When she stepped back out, Julie was buttoning her shirt. Unlike her, Julie had no problem showing a little skin and would never resort to dressing in a restroom stall. Julie was truly a tall drink of water. She had long blond hair worn to her shoulders in a straight pageboy cut and her skin had a year-round summer glow. Julie was very blessed in the chest area and didn't mind putting those assets on display. Naturally, she earned more tips than most of the other waitstaff without even trying.

Julie turned around and gave her version of a wolf whistle. "You look hot in that, Claire. I think we can find one of these rich guys for you tonight. Just give that junk in the trunk an extra wiggle!"

"You're a nut." Claire laughed. She wondered how it could be that all her female friends seemed to be in heat and always looking for a fast fix-up for her. She walked to the mirror to touch up her makeup and hair. "How is Kyle doing?"

Julie had the special smile she wore when talking about her son. "He's doing really well and asked if you'd be here tonight. He misses you."

"I miss him, too. I would be happy to watch him for you anytime. He's such a pleasure to be around."

"Thanks, Claire. I appreciate it. He's doing well in school, and the teacher there thinks he's really advanced for his age group. My kid may be the future Bill Gates and take his mother away from all this!"

"Hey, don't forget me if that happens. I could be your overpaid assistant, right?" she teased.

"You bet. It's a deal. You know I would share the wealth."

"Do you know anything about the bachelor in question for this party tonight?"

"Just that his name is Winthrop, and he has some numbers at the end so that means spoiled snooty rich kid who is marrying probably equally spoiled girl named something like Buffy or Miffy."

"You're bad, Julie." Claire looked in the mirror and tried to tame her mass of auburn hair into something manageable. She longed to put it up in a clip for a neater look, but Pam didn't like the cake girl popping out with her hair in a bun. She'd made it clear that the schoolteacher look wasn't a turn-on. Instead Claire thought the cake girl with her hair in disarray probably popped out looking like Cousin Itt from the Addams Family.

She gave a disgusted sigh, and Julie looked over and said, "I would kill for your hair. I don't know why you'd ever want to put it up. It's so sexy down." Giving her best leer, Julie said, "Babe, I would almost do you."

Claire laughed, nearly blinding herself with the mascara wand. "You must be kidding. I love your hair—it always looks so neat."

"Ugh, *neat* is another word for boring," growled Julie. "I want the wavy, sexy look that you're rocking tonight. Give me some of that curl, girl!"

Even though she thought that Julie was kidding, she did feel better about herself as she applied her lipstick. She took a last look in the mirror and thought, *Well, damn. Maybe there's hope for me after all! I bet Jason would be surprised to see me now. Wow! How did Jason come into this?* Flustered to be thinking of her boss and actually wondering what he would make of her appearance was a bit of a shock to her. Since when did her carpet-burn fantasy carry over into her after-hours life? Apparently she'd been under more stress lately than she had realized if she was now starting to have some sort of fantasy life where Jason was the star 24-7.

She needed to get this weekend behind her and return to her normal routine, where Jason was the boss she only lusted after during work hours. *Well, didn't care much.* Or how his eyes sparkled or whether he thought she was attractive. She looked over and noticed Julie giving her a questioning look.

"Did you say something?"

"Just asked if you were almost finished," Julie replied. "You seemed like you were a million miles away with some interesting thoughts."

Claire quickly assured Julie she was just worrying

about her mother. From the look on Julie's face, there was no way she bought that excuse, but she was polite enough to let it go. Claire grabbed her cover-up from her bag, pulling it on as she walked out into the hallway to call home before the party started.

Hearing Louise's voice on the other end of the line, she smiled and said, "Hey, Louise, it's me. How are you?"

"Oh, hey, honey, are you home?"

"No, I'm still in Columbia. I'll be home sometime tomorrow afternoon. How is mom doing today?"

"Oh, you know, honey. She has moments where she's living in the here and now and others where she's living in the past. Today has been in the past, mostly," Louise said sadly. "Physically though, she feels good. We sat outside on the porch for a bit this morning and enjoyed our coffee before the day got so hot, and she really loved that."

"That's great. Do you think I should try to talk to her?"

"Honey, if you want to, I'll get her, but I think it will just confuse her today since she'll assume you're Chrissie and you won't be here in person to try to calm her if she gets upset."

"Okay, Louise. I don't want you to have to deal with that, so would you just please tell her that I called when she's more lucid?"

"I will, honey. Don't you worry about us and try to have yourself a good time for once."

"Thanks, Louise. I'll see you guys tomorrow when I get home if it's not too late." She ended the call and gathered her composure. *Time to put your game face on.*

Jason settled back into the seat of the car they'd hired for the evening. With everyone expected to consume alcohol at Harold's bachelor party, Jason had made the call to hire a car to ensure that no one was driving afterwards. The noise level in the car was steadily rising as the others were picked up at their hotel, and the rare guys' night out, especially for those who were married with children, was kicking into full gear.

Jason was surprised when his thoughts turned to his assistant. In the time that she had worked for him, he had never seen her as a desirable woman. Hell, he hadn't noticed her appearance, period. When he had walked into her room after hearing a crash today and saw her standing there with wild auburn hair cascading down her shoulders and those green eyes flashing he had lost his train of thought.

He was rarely surprised by anything in life anymore, but when he felt himself getting hard while looking at her injury after her first mishap had damn near stunned him speechless. He had discreetly arranged his jeans to hide his growing reaction to her nearness. The tight confines of the bathroom had made that challenging, to say the least.

After he'd made a hasty departure from the bathroom, he took the time before lunch to take some deep breaths and tried to get back under control. He tried to tell himself that it was just a normal reaction to being near a female in close confines, and he had managed to get through lunch and the afternoon with only a few curious and confused looks across the desk at her.

Then when he had run into her in the hall this evening, all his theories had been blown away. Again, his body had an almost immediate reaction to her presence, and again he was trying to shift himself around like a schoolboy. He probably would not have noticed if her hair had been on fire most days at the office, and now this weekend he was getting an erection every time she walked in the room. Apparently it had been far too long since his last night with a woman, and he vowed to take care of that as soon as he returned home.

The party was to start at seven and generally the cake was rolled in at nine after drinks and canapés had been served. Claire worked in the kitchen for the first part of the evening. Pam thought some of the surprise was taken out of the evening if the cake girl was seen ahead of time. She wore a long apron over her cover-up as she arranged trays for the servers and ran any errands that might be needed. By eight, the party seemed to be in full swing and trays of delicious food were leaving the kitchen and returning empty at a rapid pace. It was usually a welcome sign when the guests were enjoying food at the same pace as their drinks. It seemed to keep down the number of overly intoxicated men.

As the time neared for the big cake performance, she began to get nervous, as usual. Being the center of attention was never something she desired and for those moments when she popped out of the cake, she was very much in the spotlight. As she almost always did, she thought that maybe she could just tell Pam she would be a waiter during the parties and have someone else take over the cake. The main problem with that thought was the difference in the money. Her pay for the evening was almost double that of the waitstaff and, although that might not seem like a lot to some people, it was a small fortune to her.

After loading her final tray for a server, she went to the restroom to freshen up and begin preparations for being loaded into the cake. Pam had a couple of young college men who assisted her into the cake. Brian and Max were a lot of fun and always made her laugh as they hoisted her up to the top. They'd also be the ones who wheeled the cake in and helped her down during the party in a much grander manner than the tricks they tried to pull when loading her in. Claire swatted at Brian as he tried to get Max to help him toss her like a cannonball. She laughed as they finally got her to the top of the cake, and she stepped down into the small opening.

If they could build skyscrapers and bridges spanning miles, they should surely be able to build a cake with a bottom door to avoid having to be lifted to the top. Brian and Max were always asking if maybe she'd gained a pound or two as they mocked staggering trying to lift her. She checked the top of the cake to make sure there would be no mishaps with it opening, and then she settled in.

The increase in the noise level told her that they had entered the main room of the party and she tried to settle the nervous butterflies in her stomach. The music cued up and she listened for the tap from Brian that would signify it was time for her to pop the top of the cake. He signaled and she took a big breath and jumped through the top with her arms held high above her head to much enthusiastic applause.

The honoree of the party was always seated directly in front of the cake and, taking a moment for her eyes to adjust to the light, she started to focus on that seat. Blinking her eyes, she became aware that Jason's friend Harold was standing in front of the chair of honor with Jason standing to his right. Harold was laughing and applauding while his friends around him clapped him on the back, everyone except Jason, who seemed to be studying her intently as if she were someone he was trying to place in his memory. Harold seemed to have no clue as to who she was.

The time that she was required to remain standing seemed endless as she tried to keep her head averted to avoid looking directly at Harold or Jason. She tried to act normal but was desperate to leave the spotlight before she was recognized. She turned to the side and signaled to Brian and Max to lift her down on the left side instead of the normal front position.

They were confused at the change but quickly repositioned themselves to assist with her dismount. She walked to the left of Harold to give him a hug from behind with the usual congratulations. She tried to exit the area as soon as possible to avoid looking in Jason's direction. Finally a path parted for her and she made her way to the restroom with the sound of applause following her.

Jason was completely and utterly dumbfounded. Unless his eyesight, and possibly his mind as well, was playing tricks on him, his assistant had jumped out of a cake at his best friend's bachelor party wearing next to nothing. He had been paying little attention when the cake had been rolled out and only just glanced over when the sound of the top of the cake popping open had caught his attention.

If not for seeing Claire at Harold's with her hair arranged much as it was now, he might have possibly missed what his eyes seemed to be telling him. His demure, mostly genderless assistant was actually a drop-dead bombshell, and even if it took his mind several minutes to accept it, his body knew as soon as he laid eyes on her.

How in the hell had he been so blind to her all of these years and, more important, how did one not know that his assistant jumped out of cakes at bachelor parties after work hours? She lived a whole other life outside the office, which might be normal for everyone to some degree; however, this seemed a little extreme. His little mouse of an assistant was a stripper?

He was sure that seeing her with two heads would have surprised him a lot less. Harold didn't seem to recognize her at all and was, at present, receiving well wishes from the others at the party. Comments of the more lewd variety about Claire were flying. For some reason, he wanted to protect her virtue and start punching someone in the face. He stalked angrily toward the direction in which he had seen her disappear.

Claire leaned against the restroom stall, shaking. How could this have possibly happened and why didn't she make a connection that this could be Harold's party? Julie had said the name was Winthrop, and she'd never given it another thought. She hoped against hope that she was wrong and that Jason hadn't recognized her. She began undressing and vowed to stay in the kitchen the rest of the evening, no matter what.

Dear God, she would lose her job with Jason over this. He would never understand why it was necessary to work this job as well as for Danvers. Panic started to set in and she was shaking so hard her fingers fumbled as she tried to unsnap her garters. At just that moment, she heard the door open.

"Julie, give me a few minutes. I'm having a hard

time with these darn snaps." Not thinking anything of the silence, she continued on. "God, Julie, you will never believe what just happened. My boss and his friends were at this party. I thought you said the bachelor's name was Winthrop. I need to stay in the kitchen for the rest of the evening and steer clear of Jason." As those words were uttered, she was suddenly aware that Julie hadn't made a single reply. She looked up and was looking into the blue eyes that had haunted her all day.

Time seemed to freeze as she slowly became aware that she was standing in the ladies' restroom practically naked with her boss leisurely lowering his gaze to the corset that barely contained her breasts. She could feel her nipples standing up and saluting. His gaze lowered to the skimpy matching panties and, heaven help her, she could feel her body continue to betray her as heat pooled between her thighs. She squeezed her legs together to try to control the fire that seemed to be spreading through her body like an inferno. She finally gathered her wits enough to sputter, "Wh-what're you doing in here? This is the ladies' restroom."

"I thought I would visit with the stripper for the evening. How much for a private lap dance for my friends and myself?"

"Wha . . . what?" she stammered. "What do you mean?"

"Well, you're the stripper who jumped out of the cake, correct?"

"No. No, I'm not a stripper. I just jump out of the cake with clothes on. I don't strip!"

"Clothes, huh? I'm not sure that qualifies as clothing," Jason replied with sarcasm dripping from his voice.

It finally dawned on her that she was still standing in a restroom with her boss, almost naked. She averted her eyes from his and tried to cover herself with her hands. "Could you please leave? I need to dress and this is the ladies' restroom." She made the mistake of looking up into Jason's eyes and could feel herself melt. Heat blazed there and with a muttered oath, Jason gripped her arms and dragged her against his hard body.

She went rigid at the sudden contact and tried to pull back as she felt Jason's palms start gliding lightly up her arms, leaving a trail of fire as they settled on either side of her face, his thumb gently rubbing her bottom lip. By this point, she had given up any thought of getting free and was mesmerized by the smoldering look in his eyes. As if almost against his will he leaned forward and gently laid his lips against hers. His tongue took up the course of his thumb and slowly began stroking her bottom lip. Her heart racing and her nipples turning to stone, she went boneless and sagged into him.

Jason took this as a sign of surrender and suddenly deepened the kiss, his tongue thrusting into her mouth. Startled at the sudden invasion, a brief moment of reality started to intrude but was quickly clouded as a hot masculine hand slid down her back and firmly cupped the cheeks of her bottom, bringing her into close contact with a hard bulge.

Realizing that she had the power to excite someone like Jason to this degree gave her a sense of heady intoxication as she allowed herself to be firmly molded to his body. Teeth and lips nipping and licking their way down her neck, she felt his hand cup the mound of her breast, his thumb slowly flicking the hard nipple through the lace of her corset. "Oh, Jason, please!" she cried.

"What do you want, baby? Tell me."

She wanted nothing more than to free the hard bulge from his pants and wrap her legs around his hips. She ran her hand down to the butt that she'd admired for so long and pulled him tightly against her, wrapping her ankle around his to bring their bodies even closer together. Jason raised his mouth back to hers and thrust his tongue inside as his hips thrust against hers, mimicking the action of his tongue. Just as her hand went to the snap of his jeans, a third voice in the room was heard.

"Well, well, this restroom is certainly getting a lot more interesting!" She felt Jason stiffen as she looked over in a daze and met the amused gaze of Julie. "I wondered what was keeping you, and now I see you have a very good reason for taking so long," Julie said, laughing.

Claire felt her face flame with embarrassment at being caught making out in a restroom like a teenager. She jerked away from Jason and ran into one of the stalls. As the sound of a door slamming reverberated through the restroom, she could only hope it was him leaving so she could quietly die of mortification.

"The coast is all clear, girl. Now, tell me who that hunk was and don't leave out a single juicy detail."

"Could you hand me my clothes?" Claire mumbled. Cracking the door of the stall, she took the clothes Julie handed her and dressed quickly. She knew she couldn't put Julie off any longer, so she opened the door and stepped out to see amusement still lingering in Julie's eyes.

As her eyes started to tear up, the amusement left Julie's face, and she walked over and put her arms around her. "What's going on, Claire?"

"You would not believe it, even if I told you."

"Try me. Very little shocks me. Brian said something upset you during the routine tonight and you took off as fast as you could. Would that something be the hot guy who just left?"

"That's my boss at Danvers, Jason Danvers."

Julie took a moment to digest this and said, "Okay, so your boss is here tonight. Did you know that ahead of time?"

"No, I wouldn't have worked this party knowing I could be risking my job at Danvers," she cried. "I never even gave a thought to the fact that Jason was spending the weekend with his friend Harold for his bachelor party, and you said the bachelor's name was Winthrop."

"Oh, honey, that's his last name. The name is Harold Winthrop."

She realized that she never actually knew Harold's last name and sighed.

Julie asked, "So what exactly led to the restroom scene I walked in on?"

"I recognized Jason and Harold when I jumped out of the cake. Harold didn't seem to know me, but I could see Jason possibly did. That's the reason for the change in the routine. I made sure to keep out of the direct line of sight from Jason and I really hoped he would not be able to place me. I came straight back here to change and heard the door and thought it was you. Things really got out of hand and I don't even know how it happened."

"Have you and Jason been sleeping together?"

"No, of course not. I've never even been attracted to him." Okay, so that was somewhat of a lie.

"How could you be alive and not be attracted to that hunk? And from where I was standing the feeling looked mutual."

"I'm afraid I might have lost my job tonight. He'll surely fire me."

"For what? It takes two, and he was just as guilty as you if we're taking names here. I'll cover for you if you want to leave."

"No, I'll work in the kitchen. Though, if it's okay

with you, just give me a minute to freshen up." Giving her another sympathetic look, Julie left the restroom.

Jason shut the door to the restroom and was glad to escape the prying gaze of Claire's coworker. In another few minutes, he would have taken Claire right there against the restroom wall. How could he have possibly overlooked how beautiful she was? Had he never noticed it during the time she worked for him? Apparently he was way too preoccupied at work. Under the shapeless, drab-colored clothing was a body any man would kill to possess. Her response, although timid at first, had literally blown him away, and her passion seemed to burn as hot as his.

Was his mouse of an assistant really an experienced woman of the world and a stripper to boot? Although, admittedly, she'd not stripped, but the line between being a stripper and jumping out of a cake at a bachelor party seemed pretty fine, if you asked him. Surely this violated something in her employment contract. Although this didn't qualify for the noncompete clause, this must be an ethics violation.

The thought of firing her and probably never seeing her again strangely held little appeal for him. If she valued her job with Danvers International, she would simply terminate this side job. A strong, unexpected wave of something curiously like jealousy ripped through him at the thought of men looking at her jumping out of that absurd cake at parties such as this one. He would take care of this immediately and heaven help any of his friends who had the bad fortune to make any other lewd comments about her body tonight. From this day forward, Claire would find that weekends at Danvers were a requirement that would leave her little time for anything else.

Claire made it into the kitchen without running into Jason again. She'd almost expected him to be waiting for her outside the restroom, but the coast was all clear. Julie pressed a glass of something strong and fiery into her hand and told her to drink up. Alcohol was something Claire almost never consumed, and this particular one brought tears to her eyes, but, as instructed, she finished it completely. The burn of the drink in her stomach seemed to settle it and her nerves. Julie refilled her glass again, and soon Claire was feeling much better, although maybe a little light-headed. She was also quite certain she was actually giggling.

All her worries about Jason seemed to melt away, and she was enjoying joking around with the waiters as they came into the kitchen for their next tray. Distantly she was aware that she'd just finished her third drink . . . or her fourth, and that maybe she should slow down since it would soon be time to drive home.

Finally the party started to finish up, and she gathered her stuff to walk out with Julie. They always escorted each other for safety. She felt herself stumbling on her walk to the car. "Claire, I think I need to drive you home. You're in no condition. Hey, Max lives in the Columbia area. You can catch a ride with him. Stay right here while I go talk to him." She assured Julie she would not move and leaned against the car, waiting for her friend to return.

She saw a figure walk toward her and, in her alcohol-induced haze, assumed it was Max. She walked toward him with an apology on her lips for the inconvenience of the ride and came to an abrupt halt when she recognized not Max but Jason instead. She stared at him with what could only be described as a deer-in-headlights expression. "I thought you were already gone."

"We're parked across the road and it's taking a while to get everyone together to leave since a few of the guys have had too much to drink. It looks like you have the same problem. As we're both going back to Harold's, I assured Julie that I would see you home."

"B-but you can't," she stammered. "What about your own car?"

"Since alcohol would be involved, my friends and I rented a car and driver for the evening, as anyone responsible would do." Her cheeks burned at the not too subtle insinuation that she was not responsible. She still stood silently, hesitant to get into the car even though it looked churlish to refuse.

Jason seemed to take her silence for agreement and, placing his hand on her elbow, effectively steered her toward the passenger seat of her small car. He settled her in the front seat with instructions to buckle up. He shut the door and went around to the driver's side and was forced to adjust the seat before he could fit into the car. The compact size of the car brought them into much closer proximity than she was comfortable with. She reluctantly handed her keys over to him and settled herself as close to her door as she could for some much-needed breathing room.

Chapter Seven

She remained quiet as Jason drove her small car with ease down the empty streets. The silence was finally broken when Jason sardonically asked, "So, not only do you strip, you also have a drinking problem?"

She jerked upright indignantly, replying, "I told you, I'm not a stripper, and I certainly don't have a drinking problem. If you must know, that part is *your* fault!"

"I'll play along. How is your drinking my fault?"

"If I'd not been upset from you groping me in the women's restroom, I would not have resorted to alcohol to settle my nerves," she replied hotly.

Seeing Jason's mouth tighten into a hard line, she feared she may have gone too far in her defense, but what could he expect? He'd accused her of being a stripper and an alcoholic all in the same sentence. "When you put it out there, Claire, you have to expect people will take you at face value. Apparently you enjoy this type of work, or you'd not spend your spare time doing it. Even going so far as to beg off work under the pretense of visiting family," continued Jason.

The silence after that last comment seemed to linger as if he was waiting for her to defend herself. Her stomach picked that moment to start to rebel, the nausea increasing with every moment that passed. Never being one to drink much alcohol, even in social settings, her stomach was in protest mode as the churning became harder to ignore. "Can we stop off at the next rest area please?'

"We will be back at Harold's soon. Can't it wait?" Jason asked impatiently.

"No, it can't. Please pull over as soon as possible."

Jason replied in a surprisingly gentle voice, "Just hold on. There's a rest area coming up soon."

She hoped that she wouldn't cap off what was already a humiliating evening by throwing up all over her boss. *He does deserve it though.*

She was grateful to see lights ahead as they approached a rest area. As soon as Jason parked the car, she bolted from the seat and out the door.

Thankful that the area was quiet and deserted at such a late hour, she barely made it into a stall before becoming violently ill. She lost track of time as her stomach continued to heave. She was startled to feel someone behind her and realized too late that in her haste, she'd failed to latch the stall. She turned around in shock to see a concerned Jason.

"Let me help you. Do you feel like you're finished?" Jason asked quietly.

Nodding yes, she started to leave the stall when yet another wave of sickness overcame her. She jumped back to the toilet as her stomach continued to dry heave. Gentle hands held her hair and began rubbing her back. The kindness was almost her undoing. She felt like collapsing to the floor and crying. He patiently stood there soothing her and, when at last she could leave the stall, he took a wet paper towel and wiped her face. Too drained to fight it, she allowed him to help her from the restroom and to a bench near her car.

"Let's sit outside for a few moments and make sure you're ready to travel before we start back." She was surprised when he put his arm around her and urged her head to his shoulder. Maybe some fresh air would help settle her stomach.

Claire awoke and realized she'd fallen asleep with her head on Jason's shoulder. It embarrassed her to not only be sleeping at a rest area but also sleeping off a hangover on her boss's shoulder. She was grateful the darkness hid the color she could feel creeping up her cheeks. *Great, not only does my breath smell like a dead cat, but I probably drooled all over his shirt as well.*

"Are you feeling better? It's probably not very safe to continue lingering here in the dark if you're ready to travel again."

"I—I'm fine," she said as she tried to smooth her rumpled and stained clothing as best she could. Only being able to imagine her appearance now, she hoped this whole evening was simply a bad dream that she would wake up from soon. Jason effortlessly steered back into traffic and she hoped that her stomach would hold for the rest of the trip.

"So how long have you been in this, shall we say, line of work, Claire? Was this a childhood dream of yours or something you just lucked upon later?"

So much for the softer side of Jason I witnessed at the rest area. This sarcastic question left no doubt as to whom she was dealing with. She tried her best to ignore the question, turning her head toward the window and letting the silence lengthen.

"How does one get into stripping anyway? I've always found those life choices fascinating."

She replied angrily, "I told you I'm not a stripper! I work for a party-planning company. I don't strip! Why must you continue to harp on that? I think that even you'd notice the difference between someone wearing clothes and someone nude."

"Oh, do excuse me. I apologize for the misunderstanding. I'm sure you can see how confusing it would be to see your assistant jump out of a cake at a bachelor party in a gentlemen's club. Then be driving her home because she's intoxicated outside of the club. Does any of this sound in the least unusual to you?"

"You're not my mother. I don't have to explain or justify my actions to you!" Claire replied hotly.

"Actually, that's where you're wrong. You're my assistant and, as such, you're a representative of Danvers

International, as well as a representative of me personally. How do you think this would look to our customers if, heaven forbid, one of them happens to be at a party where you're performing?"

"That's not likely to happen," she snapped.

"You never expected to see my best friend and me there tonight, either, did you? That just shows how small the world truly is."

"You can't fire me for having outside employment. My contract only states working for direct competition, and I think we can safely rule out that being a problem."

"If you'd bothered to read your entire contract, you'd find a section about behavior unbecoming of an associate of Danvers, and I feel sure that stripping would indeed fall into that category," he replied drily.

For probably the first time in her life, she felt entirely capable of violence against another. Having to sit beside Jason in the tight confines of her car while he labeled her as a stripper once again was enough to make someone as calm and mild mannered as her want to reach across the seats and slap him on his smug face. She was in no shape to fight this battle with him tonight and win, so she settled down farther in the seat and closed her eyes, pretending to sleep.

Luckily he seemed to be willing to let the matter drop for now. No doubt he was busy thinking up his next reference to stripping. She fearfully wondered what she would possibly do if he was correct about her contract, and she doubted very seriously that he was bluffing.

She was barely making ends meet now with both jobs, and there was no way she would be able to find another part-time job with the flexible hours and generous pay that Partiez Plus provided. Without the extra income, she would be forced to sell her mother's home and find a live-in facility for her. The tears gathered in the corners of her eyes, and she prayed that he wouldn't notice.

Jason was powerless to stop the self-righteous comments that continued to flow from his mouth. Even though he seemed to have no shortage of disparaging remarks to make to her, he was still reeling from the evening. The shock of realizing that the beautiful, sexy, sultry woman that he was unable to take his eyes off when she'd popped out of the cake was, in fact, his assistant, had just blown him away. Never one to spare more than a passing glance at women he considered too obvious, he had been completely captivated when Claire looked at him after jumping from the cake.

He knew those green eyes. He knew the curve of her face, and his body seemed to put it all together before his mind could catch up. The most surprising aspect had been the protective instinct that had almost immediately kicked in along with the recognition. He wanted to run up and drag her behind him until he could cover her up. He wanted to punch anyone in the crowd that dared to look at her, including his friends.

Who would have thought that he would be standing in a bathroom stall with his assistant, holding her hair back while she retched? At that moment, with her obviously in distress, all he'd wanted to do was take care of her, make every bad thing in her life disappear. She was so small and trusting curled against his chest while she slept at the rest area. This certainly was a night of firsts for him.

Sparing a quick glance at her, he was surprised to see a small hand reach up to her face and quickly wipe what appeared to be a tear from her cheek. *Good job, Jason. Way to make a lady cry.* Feeling something inside his chest clench, Jason vowed to find out more about this other life that his assistant was living. Who was the real Claire, and why was he suddenly so desperate to have that question answered?

When they finally arrived at Harold and Liz's home, she asked the question that had been on her mind for the last minutes of their trip. "Are you going to say anything to your friends about tonight?"

"No," Jason replied tightly. "I think the less they know the better. You go straight up when we get in the house, and I'll make up something to pacify them and no one will be the wiser." Greatly relieved, she murmured a quiet thank-you and followed him to the door. There was no sign of anyone in the foyer as she made her way up the stairs as quietly and quickly as possible.

She stepped inside her bedroom and went straight

to the bathroom. She quickly peeled off her clothing and stepped into the steaming shower. With a moan, she closed her eyes and let the events of the evening fall away. She eased into the shower seat and laid her head back, able to relax for the first time in hours; the steam from the shower caused her eyes to become heavy and hard to hold open.

Suddenly cold air rushed into the shower as the door was jerked open, and she was again in the bathroom with her boss. "What're you doing in here?" she shrieked.

"I was waiting in your room to make sure you were okay, and when it became apparent that you weren't coming out and there was no noise coming from here other than the shower, I thought you might have fallen and hurt yourself. Do you know how irresponsible it is to sleep in the bath or, heaven forbid, in the shower?"

"Well, add it to the long list of things about me that you find irresponsible! Let's see, there's my stripping, my drinking, and now my sleeping in the shower. Is there anything else you want to add to that tonight?" She knew she was starting to get hysterical, so she jumped up, determined to get out of the shower and away from his prying eyes.

Too late. She felt her feet start to lose their grip on the slick shower floor and, flinging her arms out, was desperate to find something to break her fall. She felt pain shoot through her hip as it connected with the seat she'd just been sitting on. Strong arms were suddenly around her and she was being lifted from the shower and cradled against a hard chest.

Despite her protests, Jason gently deposited her onto a chair in the bedroom and quickly went back to the bathroom for her robe and towel. She grabbed the robe from his outstretched hand and tried to put it on without standing and giving him a better view of her naked body. With a muttered oath, he pulled her into a standing position and slid the robe on her arms and belted it around her waist. When this was completed to his satisfaction, he pushed her back down into the chair and began drying her hair with the towel.

"I can take it from here, Jason," she said as she tried to get the towel from his hands.

"Just sit still for a minute. We don't need yet another mishap to add to the evening."

Angrily she replied, "There wouldn't have been a mishap if you hadn't barged into the bathroom, yet again. Were you raised in a barn?"

"If you were more responsible, I wouldn't have to check the bathrooms to look after you. I'm sorry for startling you, though."

Since she knew that the admission must have cost him, she decided to let the matter drop. As her boss dried her hair while she sat in front of him in nothing but a thin robe, she had to wonder when exactly she'd lost control of this weekend. What would happen to her if she lost her job with Danvers over this whole mess? Jason was not one to tolerate any excuses or anything that disrupted the smooth flow he preferred at work. Even if she was none of the things that he currently believed she was, she'd little hope of ever getting him to believe it. Maybe her only option was to throw herself on his mercy, if that existed.

"There, I believe that's close to dry. How's your hip feeling? You don't feel as if anything is broken, do you?"

"No, it's sore, but I'll be fine. Thank you. Jason," she began tentatively, "I want to explain about tonight and the nature of my job with Partiez Plus."

He ran his hand through his hair wearily and said, "Claire, we will talk about all of this tomorrow. I've reached my limit tonight, and if you insist on doing this now, I'm not certain the outcome will be what you'd hoped."

She felt greatly relieved to end the evening while still technically employed, so she quickly agreed. "Okay, tomorrow then." She jumped up from the chair, and in her haste tripped on the edge of the robe and landed in a startled heap again his chest. Her cheeks began to flame in embarrassment at displaying yet more of her clumsiness. Suddenly, his hands slid to her shoulders as if to help her. Looking up into those beautiful blue eyes, she felt her whole body come to life for the second time that evening.

As Jason started to pull her closer, she suddenly remembered that she hadn't brushed her teeth before getting in the shower. Not willing to risk letting him close enough to realize that, she stiffened and pulled back. Still holding on to her, he seemed to be fighting an internal battle before almost reluctantly setting her away from him with a curt, "Sleep well, Claire. I'll see you in the morning."

She couldn't help but feel a little lonely as the door closed quietly behind him. After brushing her teeth and finding her nightgown, she gratefully settled between the cool sheets. The room was spinning slightly as she closed her eyes, and she hoped that somehow she would be able to sleep that night.

Chapter Eight

Claire was shocked to see from the bedside clock that it was 9:00 a.m. Pain pounded in her temples as she stumbled out of bed and to the bathroom. She cringed at the image looking back at her from the mirror. Hair sticking out at all angles, dark circles under her eyes—she looked exactly like someone with a hangover. *Well, hello beautiful.* She grabbed a towel and made quick work of her shower, knowing Jason would be ready to work at any moment.

She returned to the bedroom for fresh clothing and was again brought up short by Jason standing in her room. "What're you doing in here? Do you pick locks now?"

"The connecting door wasn't locked. Big oversight on your part." Even in her current state of undress, as well as being generally pissed off that he had once again violated her privacy, she couldn't help but notice how good he looked.

Despite probably having no more sleep than she, he

looked well rested and fresh. Another pair of low-slung faded jeans and a polo shirt made him look good enough to eat. *Wonder if I could get a coffee with those sweet buns on the side?* She tried to inject disdain into her voice, asking, "Do you mind? I would like to get dressed."

"No, I don't mind at all. Please go right ahead." His amused look made her want to take off her towel and choke him with it.

"I thought we'd have breakfast in my room this morning while we work. It might be less awkward for you than having to lie to Liz and Harold about your evening with your long-lost aunt." Despite the sarcasm dripping from his voice, she was indeed happy to avoid the prying eyes of Liz and Harold and gratefully jumped at the opportunity.

"Is Liz here in the same house as Harold with the wedding today?"

"Yes, she has the top floor and Harold the bottom. I believe she's gone to get her hair done or whatever women do before the wedding now."

"Oh, okay. I'll be dressed in ten minutes. Er . . . thank you." He gave her a leisurely look from head to toe, lingering on where the short towel ended. He flashed her a rare smile and headed back through the connecting door.

At this rate, I'll never be able to be in a bedroom again without expecting my boss to come barging in the door. She pulled out a pair of jeans and a soft green tunic and then returned to the bathroom to dry her hair, fixing it in the usual weekend ponytail. With a dab of lip gloss and a light coat of concealer to hide the dark circles under her eyes, she was as ready as she was going to be. As she pushed open the door and walked into Jason's room she refused to allow herself time to worry about whether this would be her last day of employment with Danvers.

"Have a seat, Claire, and help yourself to whatever you'd like from the tray." She was impressed to see that the tray contained coffee, juice, and a variety of pastries. "I thought you might prefer a lighter breakfast after your late night." Refusing to be drawn into that conversation, she fixed herself a cup of coffee and liberally added the cream that had been provided. She selected a croissant and lowered herself into a chair, taking a grateful sip of the coffee. She looked up to find him studying her with what appeared to be real curiosity. She could feel her cheeks go red as she waited for some snide comment about her being a stripper.

"This croissant is wonderful. Surely Liz didn't take the time to do this today?"

"No. The caterer for the wedding also provided a buffet for breakfast. I fixed a tray for us to enjoy while we were working."

"Thank you. It's great."

"We've a lot to finish this morning, and I have to leave for the wedding around noon." He was probably going to wait until Monday to fire her at the office.

Maybe he would have security escort the alcoholic stripper to her car to ensure she didn't swipe anything on the way out. When she finished the last of her croissant, she powered up her laptop and began work. He handed her a list of revisions that he had made by hand on the contract, and she soon lost herself in the tedious task.

"Claire, I've a few more changes that I didn't include." Jason's breath was suddenly on her neck as he leaned over her shoulder to point out the first change. She couldn't stop herself from inhaling the erotic scent of his cologne. *Mmmm, he smells soooo good. I wonder if I can get a bottle of that cologne, pour it on my sheets, and roll in it every night.* She tried hard to continue working without Jason becoming aware of how much his closeness was affecting her. She shifted as close to the desk as she could to put some much-needed space between them. The more she shifted, the closer he shifted until she was practically lying on her laptop.

Could he possibly be doing this on purpose? She risked a quick backward glance to find those blue eyes twinkling down at her, trying to look innocent. Despite herself, she couldn't contain the laughter that bubbled out of her. "If we keep going, the desk and computer are going to end up in the floor."

Jason threw his head back and laughed as well. "I thought I would see how far you were willing to go to avoid me." This seemed to break the ice between them, and they worked in companionable silence for the next couple of hours.

She had to admit that she was surprised by his mood today. She'd expected a repetition of the previous night's insults, with possibly a termination of her employment. Instead he was acting as if nothing unusual had happened. He actually seemed more relaxed and comfortable with her. They rarely joked around at the office, but here he seemed like a different person. She desperately needed to know where her employment stood with Danvers but was afraid to broach the subject and ruin the good mood that he was in. She decided to let it go for now, hoping that Jason had decided to put the whole incident behind them. She finished up the last revision and looked over to see that Jason also appeared to be finishing up.

"If you're finished, go ahead and pack up your computer, and we'll continue in the office on Monday."

"I thought you needed to get this contract back to Mericom today."

As he leaned back in his chair, he focused those beautiful eyes on her and said, "No, there are more issues to address than I'd originally thought. This will probably run a few months until it closes." *Then why in the hell are we working this weekend? I could have saved myself a boatload of embarrassment if we had left this until Monday.*

She tried to hide the anger in her voice as she asked what she'd been thinking. "Why the need to work on it this weekend if we're months out?"

As he started packing his briefcase, Jason replied,

"As you know, we've a couple of important deals in the works that will require my attention. Until we can get Mericom wrapped up, I'm afraid weekend work will be required for the foreseeable future."

"Wh-what do you mean?"

"I mean that we will be working on Saturday and possibly Sunday for the next few months at least. Even though Mericom is of course the priority right now, I also must turn my attention to the other projects we already have in the works. To do this, I'm afraid it's going to take some team effort and sacrifices on both our parts."

Jason studied her reaction to the news he had just delivered. She looked completely stunned and for once at a loss for words. No doubt she was busy running through her future stripping commitments and wondering how to postpone them. Part of him almost felt guilty for causing this apparent upheaval in her life, especially since he could easily handle all the current projects on the table and probably a few more as well. Claire, however, didn't need to know that.

If not for some last-minute issues that had come up with the merger, it would have been wrapped up today, and finding reasons to make her work on the weekends would have been a little more challenging. Even though he didn't like delays, he couldn't say he was sorry for how things had worked out. The merger would go forward—of that he was certain—but the de-

lay this time was a bonus for him. He tried not to pon-
der what his motives were in this as he finished packing
his stuff.

He risked one more covert look at her and was surprised at how disappointed he was to find her hair up
again. She looked young and vulnerable with her ponytail, like someone who looked as though they needed
to be protected from the world. He had the sudden
urge to lay his lips on the pulse beating in the curve of
her neck.

When he had been standing behind her earlier, the
floral scent of her skin had intoxicated him. What
started as a playful game had fast turned a corner for
him. He'd had to pull back and hope to walk to the
other seat without her noticing the sudden tent in the
front of his jeans.

He seemed to have lost all of his poise and polish
this weekend. Instead he was back in high school trying to control his hormones and avoiding, as they said
back then, "having a boner all weekend long." With a
grimace, he stood up and jolted Claire out of the fog
that she'd been in since his announcement of the weekend work requirement.

Claire looked up as Jason rose from the desk and began
packing his suitcase. She wondered how to broach the
subject of the weekend work again without angering
him and jeopardizing her job. *You have until next weekend to work something out with him; just let it go for now*

and worry about it later. She stood and packed her side of the desk up and walked quickly toward the connecting door.

"Claire." Hearing her name, she turned to look at Jason inquiringly. "I told Harold that I would be downstairs soon. He and the other guys are in the room at the back of the house, and with Liz gone right now, you should be in the clear if you'd rather leave and avoid saying good-byes."

Overcome with relief and gratitude, she said a heartfelt, "Thank you. I really appreciate it," and quietly left the room.

Even though she felt sure that Harold and Liz didn't know what had happened last night, she was still grateful to avoid seeing them when she left. She quickly gathered her clothing and toiletries and was soon packed. When she heard Jason's door close, she allowed an additional ten minutes and quietly left her room. She made her way cautiously down the stairs, relieved to see that the foyer was indeed empty. She wasted no time in loading her items into her car and heading down the drive.

She felt almost as if she were fleeing, the relief was so great when she made it down the driveway and was back on the road. To say she was puzzled by Jason's behavior was an understatement. Upon awaking this morning, she instantly imagined the talk between Jason and herself concerning the previous night. She fully expected a condescending lecture at the very least and a termination of her employment with Danvers International as the worst-case scenario. She was hesitant to think that he had decided to let the matter drop.

She didn't know what she would do if he pushed the issue of her quitting the job at Partiez Plus. The extra income barely covered her mother's medication each month. He also mentioned working on the weekends for the next few months. Luckily the bachelor parties were usually later in the evening, so she didn't foresee that being a problem; however, it would limit the amount of time she could spend with her mother on the weekends. She noticed an approaching rest area and stopped to give Louise a call.

Hearing Louise's voice on the other end of the line always brought a smile to her face. "Hey, Louise, how are you doing today?"

"Oh, honey, I'm doing just fine. These old bones are still getting me around, and the ticker is beating strong." Louise laughed.

"I'll be hearing you use that same line twenty years from now, Louise," she said with a smile.

"I don't know about that, honey, but I hope to be saying it tomorrow. One day at a time at my age, you know?"

Claire had a similar exchange with Louise on every call. Truthfully, Louise never seemed to age; she still looked the same today as when Claire first met her. "I was going to come over for dinner. Can I bring anything?"

"Honey, I don't need anything. I've got everything I need to make the homemade spaghetti you love."

"Oh, Louise, you don't have to do that, but I would be more than happy to eat it! How is mom doing today?" Hearing the pause in Louise's voice, she knew this was not a good day for her mother.

"She's fine, honey, and I'm sure she'll be happy to see you. Give her time today. She's been a bit confused."

Sighing, Claire said, "That happens so often now. Maybe I should talk to the doctor again about changing some of her medications. The last one he added seems to be making her worse."

"I don't know if that will help, honey. I think the good Lord above controls most everything for us down below," Louise replied.

She said good-bye to Louise and started back on the road, wanting to stop at her apartment for a shower and a quick nap before going to her mother's for dinner.

Chapter Nine

When she finally arrived home, she pulled into her parking spot and turned to retrieve her suitcase from the back seat. As she was straightening up she heard a voice that made her inwardly cringe. "Claire, you're back! Old Billy has scored those Neil Diamond tickets that I told you about." *No, no, NO! Please, Lord, haven't I been through enough this weekend? Please, if you make him go away I promise I'll go to church every Sunday, be kind to old people, and donate something to charity that I'm not counting on my taxes.*

As Billy smiled at her she wondered why the universe seemed to be against her this weekend. She'd not made it to her apartment in weeks without being accosted by Billy as she was leaving the car. Could he actually be in his apartment waiting for her every day? No, surely even *he* had more to do than spend hours watching for her arrival.

Giving him a tight smile, she said, "Hey, Billy, how's it going?"

"Did you hear what I said about the Neil Diamond tickets?"

"Er. . . . Yes, I heard that, but I'm sure there's someone you'd rather take than me, Billy. Maybe Melissa in four B. She loves concerts," she supplied hopefully.

"Oh no, babe, Billy got these tickets especially for you."

"Um . . . My mother is expecting me any moment at her house for dinner, so let's talk about this later," she replied as she slowly made her way around him and toward her apartment.

Billy looked down at his watch and said in obvious confusion, "It's only after three. Why would you have dinner this early?"

She tried to stick as close to the truth as possible. "She has a medical condition and has to eat several times per day, so we're eating earlier today."

Luckily, this seemed to occupy Billy's thought process long enough for her to make her way around him and to her apartment door. With a wave, she said, "I'll talk to you later." She practically ran through her front door, wincing at how loud the door slammed in her haste to escape. She wondered how much longer she would be able to live with this daily aggravation before she either hurt his feelings or she just gave up and moved.

After a weekend of looking at and *drooling over* the hot body of Jason, being pursued by Billy was a reality check. It was like having to settle for sirloin after having the prime rib. *You can't win 'em all, girl. For every hot guy you're looking for, five creepy and weird guys are looking for you.* She walked to the bedroom and set her suitcase on the floor. The light was blinking on her answering machine. She thought about not even bothering to check the messages. Hadn't she had enough bad news this weekend? Curiosity got the better of her, though, and she pushed the button and was informed that she had one new message.

"Claire, it's me, Suzy. I, um . . . Oh, Claire, Jeff and I broke up!" Hearing what was plainly a sob, she walked closer to the machine as if she could see Suzy. "He has been cheating on me. The bastard has been cheating on me with his dentist. Can you freaking believe that?!" Now openly sobbing, Suzy continued. "I . . . I'm okay; I just didn't have anyone to tell. Shit!" When the beep signaled the end of the recording, Claire stood rooted to her spot, completely stunned.

Suzy and Jeff had been together since high school and had been engaged for the last three years. Sure, everyone joked about them taking their sweet time to get married but there was never a doubt in Claire's mind that they'd spend their lives together. Jeff was the exact opposite of Suzy, quiet and serious to her loud and outgoing personality.

He seemed to dote on Suzy and she seemed to breathe life into him. Claire felt so guilty that she'd not been there for Suzy and, come to think of it, she'd not told Suzy she would be out of town, either. *Great, my friend in need thinks I bailed on her this weekend! Score: crappy weekend—3, Claire—0.*

She picked up the phone, walked into the living room, and settled herself on the couch to call Suzy. A low quiet voice answered the phone. "Hello?"

"Suz, it's me, Claire. I'm so sorry. I just got your message. I was out of town. What in the world is going on?" Suzy started to cry. Raw, seemingly uncontrollable sobs were coming so fast it was as if a dam had collapsed. "Suz, hold on. I'm coming over there right now."

"No," Suzy managed to get out between sobs. "Beth is here."

Beth was Suzy's younger sister who lived across town and worked as a schoolteacher. She knew they were extremely close and immediately felt better knowing Beth would slay dragons to protect her sister.

"Can you talk, Suz?"

Suzy took a couple of shuddering deep breaths, trying to get herself back under control. Claire held the phone in silence, giving Suzy the time she needed to compose herself. "I . . . I was just so shocked, Claire," Suzy began weakly. "I thought we were happy. We hadn't been fighting, the sex was still good, and he didn't have any of the usual signs. He wasn't late coming home, didn't switch brands of underwear and, hell, he didn't even start using hair gel," Suzy finished in disbelief.

She had no idea what hair gel had to do with infidelity. That was probably something from Suzy's bible, *Cosmopolitan*. "Suz, how do you know he's involved with someone else? Maybe he just needs some time alone?"

"I saw text messages on his phone and not the ones reminding him of his appointment, but the 'I want to stick my tongue down your throat' type. The funny thing is I was not suspicious at all. I grabbed his phone thinking it was mine since they look alike. I was scrolling through the phone looking for a number that Beth had texted me earlier. At first, I was just confused as to what all the text messages were and who Melissa was. I opened the first one, still thinking that someone had the wrong number and had sent me all those messages by mistake. I read through probably fifty messages and each one seemed to unfold a secret life and a part of Jeff that I didn't know existed.

"I was so shocked. The messages and his replies were so out of character for the Jeff I'd known all those years. When he walked back in and saw me holding the phone, he didn't even bother to make excuses. It was almost as if he was relieved that I'd found out. I swear, it was the most surreal moment of my life, and you know that's saying something."

She was glad to hear the smile she could detect in Suzy's voice and her attempt at humor when she finished her sentence. "Did he move out, Suz?"

"Yeah, the rat bastard was packed and out the door within the hour. I think he must have had the suitcase half-packed already and was waiting for the opportunity," Suzy wearily finished.

"Suz, I don't know what to say. I can't believe it. Maybe you guys can talk and try to work through things. He might just be confused, and it's possible he didn't have sex with the girl."

"Bullshit! Trust me. Without going into a lot of disgusting details, he did have sex with the slut dentist. She drilled more than a hole in his mouth, that's for damn sure."

Even clearly upset, Suzy, as usual, had a way with words. She gave new meaning to the old saying about making a sailor blush. "Are you sure you don't want me to come over there?"

"I'm not much company. I want to continue this outstanding pity party that I'm hosting for myself today. Tomorrow it's over and I'm going to forget the scumbag ever existed. So, where were you this weekend?" Suzy suddenly asked.

Claire had hoped to get off the phone before Suzy brought that up. "I had to work." In a vain attempt to change the subject, she quickly asked, "Are you feeling better?"

"Wait, you had to work all weekend? You never do weekends."

"It's the merger with Mericom. There were some important changes that had to be made this weekend, that's all," she hedged.

"You were in the office with Smoking Buns all weekend?"

"Well, um, not exactly in the office," she replied evasively.

Claire stood up and started to pace her apartment, knowing that Suzy was fixing to go off like a drill sergeant. "What do you mean, 'not exactly in the office.' Where were you exactly?"

She felt like she'd traveled back in time and was being questioned by her father after coming home late. "Um, well, I sort of went to Columbia, because Jason had to go to a friend's house for the weekend and he needed to work while he was there." Her shoulders tightened as she waited for the inevitable barrage that would certainly be coming.

"Hmm, I see. How long have you been bumping uglies with Smoking Buns, you tart?"

"I most certainly am not 'bumping uglies,' whatever that's supposed to mean. I'm not bumping anything with Jason!"

"Yeah, yeah, save it for someone who buys it. I'm going to need some details here. I mean complete disclosure, no sweaty stone left unturned. Tomorrow night we're going out to dinner after work and you're giving me the four-one-one on this whole sordid story. Don't even think about saying no—I'll drag you kicking and screaming if I need to," Suzy threatened.

She knew it was useless trying to correct Suzy, and

hearing the excitement back in her friend's voice, she decided to let her labor under the false assumption for the night. She knew that Suzy needed something else to focus on, even if the fantasy was all in her head.

"I promise I won't back out. You pick the place tomorrow. I love you Suz, and I'm here if you need me."

"I love you too. I might even tattoo your name on my rump this weekend," Suzy joked.

"You're impossible. You know that, right?" She laughed. Promising once again to go to dinner tomorrow, she was smiling as she finished the call.

Anyone else would be depressed and miserable for months over a breakup of this magnitude, but Suzy would do exactly as she said. She would be miserable for the rest of the day and tomorrow she would forge straight ahead as she put her life back together.

The drive through Myrtle Beach was slow during the tourist season. Girls in skimpy swimsuits walked down "the Boulevard," usually followed by some guys hoping for a summer fling. The water parks and putt-putt courses were doing a booming business. Claire felt much older than her twenty-eight years with the weight of so much responsibility on her shoulders. She was relieved when she made it through the heavy traffic and arrived at her mother's home.

She quickly exited the car and made her way to the door, so today she could turn a blind eye to all the repairs that were so obviously needed. Louise was waiting with the door open and a smile on her face. How would she ever survive if that smiling welcome wasn't waiting for her each time?

In a way, Louise had become more of a mother to her than her own over the last few years. With her mother's worsening Alzheimer's, there were so many days now that she barely recognized Claire, and Louise was always there to smooth the hurt away. She walked to the top of the steps and put her arms around Louise, giving her a tighter hug than usual.

Louise looked inquiringly at her. "You okay, honey?"

"I'm great, Louise, and I like the new hair color." Both burst out laughing at the same time. Louise's hair was usually brown but there was now a decidedly pink hue to it.

"You know how it goes on the hair. Sometimes you look like the girl on the box and sometimes you look like the box exploded on your head." Louise chuckled.

"Well, I think it looks great."

She saw her mother walk into the foyer and gave her a bright smile. "Hi, Mom, you look so nice today."

Her mother looked at her in confusion and asked, "Louise, do we have company?"

With a sick feeling in her stomach, she realized that her mother had no idea who she was. She walked forward slowly so as not to startle her mother and played the role she'd been forced into more and more lately. "Hi, Evelyn, it's lovely to see you again," she said as she extended a hand toward her mother.

Her mother hesitantly held her hand out, took Claire's in her own, and gave it a light squeeze.

"Evelyn, Claire is a friend who is joining us for lunch today. I hope that's okay with you." Not waiting for a reply, Louise stepped forward and gently led her mother back to her favorite chair in the living area and then continued on to the kitchen.

Sometimes it was actually easier to be a stranger to her mother rather than have to pretend she was Chrissie. These lapses of memory could last for her entire visit or her mother could slip in and out several times, which was exhausting to keep up with.

"What can I help you with, Louise?"

"I don't need any help, honey. Just have a seat and relax while I finish the sauce up." Claire took a seat on the sofa and noticed that her mother was already engrossed in watching *Family Feud*. Claire discussed the contestants with her and enjoyed seeing how animated she became, even if it was over a game show.

The spaghetti was mouthwatering, and Claire cleaned her plate and helped herself to seconds. Even being a stranger to her mother, she still enjoyed the afternoon and evening with them more than she had in quite some time. All too soon it was time to go home. She gave Louise another hug and also chanced to give her mother a quick one.

Still smiling after the enjoyable evening, she pulled into the lot of her apartment building and paused. Maybe Billy was watching her space? Deciding to use the visitor's parking at the end of the complex, she locked her car and quickly headed toward her door. There was no sign of him, and she opened her door and shut it with a feeling of triumph. Giving a big fist pump, she had to laugh at herself. Maybe her luck was changing after all.

Chapter Ten

Claire entered her office on Monday morning feeling apprehensive about what was to come. Would this be the day that Jason confronted her about her job at Partiez Plus? She would have no choice in the matter if he forced her hand. She would have to quit her job with Partiez and then look for another job to fill the income gap. She would have to work more hours to come close to matching what she made working for Pam on the weekends. Jason's door was still shut, which left her wondering if he was in yet.

She noticed a note from Jason on her desk as she slid into her seat. Quickly skimming the note, she felt a smile break out. Yes, indeed, her luck did seem to be turning: He was going to be out of the office today. The note instructed her to check her e-mail for a list of tasks that needed to be completed and that he would not be in the office until tomorrow morning.

She worked steadily all morning and only paused to grab a drink and pack of crackers out of the vending machine before getting back to work. Around 2 p.m., Suzy came breezing through the door. Claire stopped writing the e-mail she was composing and carefully studied Suzy's face. *Amazing, you'd never know what happened to her this weekend.* She looked exactly the same as she did every day. A grin tugged at her lips as she again read Suzy's T-shirt to make sure she had it right. The shirt was bright orange with Little Caesar's Pizza in small white writing at the bottom. In bold, black print, it had the slogan "Hot and Ready." She'd paired the eye-catching shirt with a pair of snug black jeans, a chain belt, and a pair of stiletto heels. Only Suzy could make an outfit like that seem perfectly normal and completely cool.

"Where's Hot Buns?"

She laughed despite herself and said, "He's out of the office today."

"So, remember we're going out to dinner tonight, right? Jeff had a little money in our joint account, so we're going to spend every last dime of it on a fancy-shmancy meal at that new restaurant, The Ivy," Suzy said with what could only be called an evil smile.

"Oh, wow, I've heard of it, but I'm not dressed for anything that fancy," Claire said regretfully.

"No worries. I've got everything covered. I brought two dresses with me today. They're hanging in my office."

"Suz, I can't wear your clothes. They'll be too short for me."

"It's a dress, silly—there's no such thing as a dress that's too short. It'll be fine. I have the matching shoes as well, and I know we both wear the same size, so we're all set."

Suzy looked so pleased with herself that Claire didn't have the heart to argue with her. If it kept that smile on Suzy's face, then she would wear a garbage bag tonight if she had to. Suzy arranged to meet her in the restroom down the hall at five, where they'd both change and leave straight from work for their six o'clock reservation at The Ivy.

She pushed SEND on her last e-mail and prepared to pack up her desk for the day. This really was an enjoyable afternoon. With Jason gone, she'd cleared up most of her backlogs of work with only a few interruptions. Noting that she had five minutes to lock up and meet Suzy, she grabbed her purse, turned off the lights, and locked the door. For security reasons, the office was always locked when they were not there. The supervisor of the cleaning crew had a key for nightly cleaning, but that was the only other person allowed in.

Suzy was already in the restroom when she arrived. "Hey, girlfriend, I have our dresses all ready. Your dress is in the pink cover so go ahead and grab that one and try it on." Suzy grabbed the leopard-skin cover-up which apparently contained her dress and walked into a stall while Claire unzipped the pink cover-up to inspect her dress. She was relieved to see that it was a dark-green silk dress, which looked innocent to her eyes. *Please, please don't let it be spandex.* She went into the other stall and slipped her clothes off and the dress on.

The dress was actually beautiful, with a pleated, strapless bodice and an Empire waist that flowed smoothly into a formfitting skirt. There were only two problems with the dress that she could see. The snug bodice showcased her assets and pushed her breasts into looking more like D-cups rather than her usual small C. The second problem was the length. The dress was well above her knees. Well, *well* above them. If she had to bend over for anything tonight it was going to get X-rated in a hurry.

She sucked it up and walked out of the stall without complaint, remembering her vow to do whatever she had to do to make sure Suzy had a good night. Suzy was leaving the next stall over and Claire realized that her cover-up bag hadn't been leopard skin after all. It was clear and the dress it contained was what Claire had seen. Only Suzy could make something that should be totally mind-boggling into something that others would actually envy.

Suzy's dress was a similar style to the one that Claire was wearing, strapless with a high bodice. Where her dress was more tailored looking, Suzy's had clear rhinestones and a sassy little ruffle at the top that showed off the curve of her ample breasts to perfection. Her dress was about the same length as Claire's.

"Hey, that dress is rocking on you," Suzy exclaimed

and then followed the comment up with a loud whistle.

She smiled, saying, "You look great, Suz; that dress is so you. This dress, however, doesn't seem like you; what gives?"

"That's Beth's dress actually; I just wanted to freak you out thinking it was one of mine. I figured your rear end would hang out of mine since they're really short on me. I had to drop Beth off at home this morning and I borrowed that one for you."

Touched that Suzy had gone to so much trouble to make sure she didn't have any excuse to get out of dinner, she smiled and didn't make any complaint. She asked Suzy to zip her dress and then stepped over to the mirror and borrowed some of Suzy's makeup.

"Hey, let me do your makeup. You need a new look with that dress." Again, deciding to let Suzy have her way tonight, Claire gave herself over to a makeover. "Okay, I'm all done and you look fantastic."

Claire could hardly connect the person staring back at her in the mirror as herself. Suzy had really applied more eye makeup than she had ever used and as a result her green eyes looked huge. Her lips were a glossy red and the blush accented her cheekbones.

"Now, take that hair down and brush it. The spinster hair with the sultry dress is a definite clash."

She released the clip from her hair and set about taming it into some form of order. Suzy took that over as well and when she was finished applying the last coat of hair spray, she had to admit that she looked good. *Maybe a bit like a classy hooker but, hey, take one for the team.* They packed up and took the elevator to the lobby. As people turned to stare at them, Claire practically ran from the building to Suzy's small SUV.

Thirty minutes later, Suzy was pulling in front of the valet stand, and the door was opened for her by a young man in a uniform. Claire noticed the attention she was receiving from the rest of the valets. Suzy walked around the car, and the admiring looks were then turned to her, and Claire was quickly forgotten. No matter where she went, Suzy was usually the center of attention, and she was more than happy to have her in that role.

"Hey, babe, take good care of my ride," Suzy said with a dramatic bat of her eyelashes. The poor guy almost fell over his feet in his haste to take the keys from her. With a wink, Suzy tossed her keys over and took off toward the entrance to the restaurant like she owned the place.

Sometimes I wish I had just half the confidence that Suzy does, she thought as she followed her to the reservation desk. Luckily for them the host was another male, and Suzy batted her lashes again and said, "Hey, reservations for two for Denton. Do you think you could possibly give us a table at the window? I just love the ocean at night; it's so sensual."

She truly felt sorry for him; he literally swallowed

his tongue in his haste to please her. "Ye . . . yes, I think I can find you something. We've a table that's reserved for 6:30, but I'm sure they wouldn't mind waiting until you ladies are finished. Come right this way."

Indeed, they were led to a table with a breathtaking view of the Atlantic Ocean. The restaurant was dimly lit and relied on candlelight from each table as well as twinkling white lights similar to Christmas tree lights to create an intimate atmosphere. The host rushed over to pull out a chair for Suzy, and Claire was left to seat herself. For such a popular place, she was impressed at how spacious the area was around each table.

"Wow, this is great, Suz. I can't believe we got such a good table."

"Yeah, this is cool. I know Jeff would want us to enjoy the evening with his money, so let's do it right. Order the most expensive item on the menu, and we're even springing for champagne," Suzy replied with obvious glee.

Laughing, she opened her menu to look at the options.

Their waiter arrived at the table, luckily another male, and in minutes their champagne had arrived and they were enjoying a glass. "I propose a toast," Suzy said. Claire raised her glass and waited for Suzy to continue. "Ummm. . . . This is for my sleazebag ex, Jeff, with the small package: May the rest of what you have between your legs shrivel even more and may the breasts of your ho-bag dentist drop to her ankles."

They clicked their glasses grandly, both dissolving in a fit of laughter.

Claire felt a tap on her shoulder and looked up expecting to see their waiter. She was shocked to see none other than Jason Danvers looking down at her with a smile on those sexy lips.

"Ladies, I couldn't help but overhear your toast. I do hope things work out as you requested, Suzy."

"Hey, Mr. D., thanks, man," Suzy replied without missing a beat. Claire was surprised that Jason actually remembered Suzy's name and equally surprised to see that Suzy was not intimidated in the least by him. She could feel herself cringing as Suzy continued. "You want to pull up a chair and join us? We could use some male company tonight."

"I couldn't think of anything that I would rather do than dine with two beautiful women. Unfortunately, I'm with Grayson Merimon tonight. Claire, you might recall that Grayson is the CEO of Mericom?" Jason's gaze had settled on her as he waited for a reply.

"Ye . . . Yes, I remember. I've never met him in person, but I do recall the name." She could feel her cheeks turning red as she felt herself stammering through her reply. *Oh Lord, he looks good enough to eat tonight. I wonder if he's on the menu because I would order that for sure.*

"Well, let's rectify that now. I'm sure Grayson would love to meet you. I hope you ladies will join us for a drink at our table?"

Already forming a polite refusal on her lips, she was

dismayed to see Suzy pop up from her seat with, "Sounds cool, Mr. D. Lead the way." She shot Suzy her best what-the-hell-are-you-doing look but had no choice but to follow them over to the table.

As they approached, a tall, striking man stood up. *Oh, baby, this guy could give Jason a run for his money in the hot category. Wow!*

"Ladies, this is Grayson Merimon. Grayson, this is Suzanna Denton—or Suzy, as we call her—who handles event planning for Danvers, and this is my personal assistant, Claire Walters."

Grayson extended a hand to Suzy first. "Ms. Denton, a pleasure to meet you."

Suzy gave his hand a quick shake and replied, "What's up, Gray?" Grayson's eyes widened slightly in surprise, a smile starting to play around his generous lips as he then turned toward Claire and extended his hand.

"Ms. Walters, after speaking with you on the telephone and via e-mail, I feel like I already know you. It's a pleasure to put a face with the voice." Grayson's hand engulfed hers in a warm grip.

"Grayson, I hope you don't mind, but I've invited Suzy and Claire to join us for a drink."

"Of course not, Jason, it would be a pleasure." Jason seated Claire and Grayson pulled out a chair for Suzy.

Claire murmured a quick thank-you and Suzy looked over her shoulder at Grayson, "Thanks, G." Again, she could see Grayson's lips twitch.

Claire felt Jason's powerful thigh touch against hers under the table and her body leapt to life in response. *Oh great, it's been so long between men that I'm going to have an orgasm just from a little leg contact.* She shifted as far away as she could and felt Jason's thigh once again brushing hers. Any more shifting and she would be out of the chair and on the floor. She was certain he was doing it on purpose. Ignoring him, she focused her attention on the conversation at the table.

Jason was explaining to Suzy that in the next few months she would be working with Grayson and his staff to put together a formal party to celebrate the merger between the two companies. Suzy was asking if they'd thought of providing some type of entertainment. Suddenly Claire became aware that the whole table was looking at her.

"Excuse me, did you say something?"

"Yes, I told Suzy that you might have some ideas for good party entertainment," Jason said, with what could only be called a wicked grin.

She was speechless for a moment, terrified that Jason was going to elaborate on what he was clearly hinting at. "I, um . . . I don't think I've any ideas about that. Suzy is the master planner. I'm sure she'll have lots ideas."

Luckily, this successfully diverted the attention back to Suzy. Without thinking, she reached over under the table and dug the heel of her shoe into Jason's foot. His thigh jerked as she continued to face forward with a smile. At that moment, the waiter approached the table and asked if they'd like to order. She opened her mouth to ask Suzy if she was ready to return to their table, trying to make her escape.

"Jason, why don't we invite these lovely ladies to join us for dinner?" Grayson asked.

With a smug look, Jason replied, "I think that's a wonderful idea, Grayson."

"Groovy, count me in, Mr. D.," Suzy said. With everyone at the table again looking at her, Claire had little choice but to accept. Suzy asked the waiter to bring their champagne over to the new table and soon they were all placing their food order.

Claire realized she'd already had two drinks and knew she'd better slow down before it went to her head. Jason made her so nervous, and more than once she could feel his gaze fixed on her. His thigh was now a permanent fixture against hers. No matter how many times she tried to shift away from him, he always managed to resume the contact within minutes. She found herself wondering how that thigh would feel between her own.

She unconsciously pressed her thigh closer to Jason's as she imagined wrapping her legs around him as he entered her. She was soon completely lost in the fantasy. A clatter in the kitchen jerked her out of her trance, and she realized that, although Suzy and Grayson continued to talk as if nothing unusual was happening, Jason's eyes were riveted on her, and she quickly discovered why. Not only were their thighs now almost inseparable, her hand was also tightly gripping his upper thigh. *Oh shit, I've felt my boss up—in public, no less—and he knows exactly what I was thinking!*

Jerking her hand away and putting distance between them again, Claire was relieved when their dinner arrived and provided a much-needed distraction. Had anyone else noticed what was going on? Jason quite obviously had but luckily Grayson and Suzy seemed clueless that she'd been groping her boss under the table.

When was the last time he had an erection at the dinner table? Maybe back in high school or college but certainly never with an important business colleague and two of his employees. Things would be damn embarrassing for him now if he had to leave the table. He had been playing with Claire all evening, teasing her about party entertainment and then moving his thigh closer to hers every time she attempted to put some space between them. When she'd suddenly pressed her thigh tightly to his and her breathing quickened, he was too surprised to move for a minute.

Still thinking it was just an accident, he was even more surprised when she left it there and then shocked when he felt a hand settle on his thigh, almost brushing against the length of him. His little assistant was quite obviously turned on, and he hoped that he was what had her so hot and bothered. He tried to keep up with the conversation from the others at the table so that attention would not be focused on what seemed to be going on between them. Was she trying to let him know that she wanted him?

He couldn't have been more shocked if she'd up-ended her glass on the top of his head. Darting a glance at her, he saw that she appeared to be deep in thought. Did she even know what she was doing to him? When she jerked against him and looked up with wide eyes, he'd felt the urge to grab her hand and drag her out of the restaurant and to his car. She acted as if she'd no idea what had just happened between them.

She quickly removed her hand and pulled away from him as far as she could. If she was dream-walking over there, he hoped it continued somewhere a little more private. He was more than willing to let her have her way with him but would like it to be somewhere that wouldn't get them both arrested. He was so turned on he could hardly stay in his seat.

She looked so beautiful tonight. Somehow, he didn't think the clothes she was wearing were actually hers, because they were far more revealing than she would normally wear. Her pale creamy breasts swelled out of the top of the dress and miles and miles of legs were on display for the world to see. Well, hell, she did jump out of a cake with next to nothing on, and even though he hated that, he could almost believe that it was just a job to her and not her normal nature.

What made that job necessary to her was a mystery he intended to solve. He hoped the erection pushing at the zipper of his slacks would subside before it was time to leave. He settled back in his chair, praying that more than his dinner would cool off soon.

Claire picked at the shrimp and tilapia she'd ordered. Conversation flowed smoothly around the table. More than once she'd caught a questioning glance directed her way from Suzy and had managed a smile of reassurance in return. Grayson was a very entertaining dinner companion and kept everyone laughing with stories from various events he had attended.

Suzy continued to be herself and made some comments that she was sure that Jason would not appreciate in front of a business associate. She, however, was surprised when instead of being offended he openly laughed along with Suzy and appeared in no way put off by her outspoken nature.

Jason's thigh returned to press against hers, and she'd given up trying to keep distance between them. She knew she'd once again had too much to drink thanks to the man beside of her. When the waiter returned to clear their plates and offer drinks and dessert, she gratefully ordered a coffee. Soon everyone was finished, and the coffee had helped lessen some of the effects of the champagne.

"Ladies, I think I also speak for Jason when I say dinner with you was a great pleasure. This is the most enjoyable meal I've had in quite some time."

"I completely agree. This has been the most, er . . .

stimulating meal I've had as well in quite some time," Jason replied with a rueful smile. She wanted to kick him under the table. She was sure his comment was directed toward her, especially the "stimulating" part.

When Jason took the check from the waiter, Suzy protested, determined to spend Jeff's money. But Jason won in the end. "Ladies, can I drop you off somewhere?" Jason asked.

"No thanks, Mr. D. My wheels are here and I'm dropping Claire back at the office to pick up her car, so we're cool."

"I'm actually running by the office myself to pick up some papers I left there, so why don't I drop off Claire and save you the trouble, Suzy?"

Claire shook her head, a polite "no thank you" on her lips when, to her shock and dismay, Suzy replied, "Hey, groovy, Mr. D. That would totally save me a trip back into town."

What in the hell has gotten into her? I'm going to strangle her when I get her alone. Not only have I felt my boss up this evening; now thanks to my best friend I have to ride with him too!

As she tried to catch Suzy's eye, she found herself instead staring at the back of her friend's head as she sailed out of the restaurant ahead of them like a queen. She followed as fast as she could, desperate to get Suzy's attention before Jason and Grayson arrived at the exit of the restaurant.

Just as she reached her and took her arm, she felt her

other arm clasped from behind and a voice in her ear, "They're bringing up my car now." Shit, she was well and truly trapped. She released Suzy's arm and settled for giving her a scathing look instead.

Suzy ignored her and instead turned to Grayson, "Talk at ya later, Gray." She reached up with her knuckle to pop Grayson on the shoulder.

Grayson looked a little surprised and vastly amused as he studied Suzy and replied, "Yes, it's been interesting, Suzanna, very interesting." Suzy appeared taken aback by the use of her full name, but, in typical Suzy fashion, she shrugged and laughed it off. Grayson turned to her and extended his hand. "Claire, it's been a pleasure. I'm sure I'll be talking to you soon."

All too quickly, Jason's sleek black Mercedes arrived at the valet station, and he held the door open for her. Accepting defeat, she slid onto the soft leather seat, and he shut the door and walked around to the driver's side. "Claire, why don't I drop you off at your home instead of at your car? It's late, so rather than navigating a dark parking lot it would probably be more feasible for both of us to call it a night."

"Bu . . . But, I don't have a way to work tomorrow. I have to get my car tonight," she protested.

Too late, she realized she'd just stepped neatly into a trap. "I'll of course be glad to pick you up in the morning as well," he replied smoothly.

"That's too much trouble. You can just drop me off at my car."

"I would prefer to see you to your door and know you have arrived home safely." Rather than persist in arguing, she quietly gave him directions to her apartment.

"So, what was the reason for the celebration tonight? I gather it had something to do with a man from the toast I overheard?"

"Mmm, yes, Suzy's boyfriend, or ex-boyfriend, Jeff."

"Bad breakup, huh?"

"You could say that. I won't go into the whole thing, but it was sudden and unexpected."

"That's a real shame. Suzy is great and I can't imagine a man doing any better," he said earnestly. He just continued to surprise her and apparently her expression showed it.

"What're you thinking?"

"I'm surprised that in a company the size of Danvers you seem to know everyone."

"They're my people, Claire. As such, each of them is important to me. Everyone there contributes to the success we have and they're as worthy of my respect and concern as are you," he added quietly.

Had she ever really known Jason? She'd always felt that he was oblivious to everything around him other than the bottom line. The truth seemed to be quite the opposite. He had his hands on everything in his company and obviously spent a lot of his time getting to know each person in it. She was surprised to see them approaching her apartment. She was almost sorry to see the ride end so quickly. She directed Jason to her vacant parking spot and let out a loud groan before thinking.

"What's the matter?"

"Oh, it's just my neighbor, Billy. I can never seem to get into my apartment anymore without him stopping me."

"Is he bothering you?" he demanded.

"It's nothing major. He just wants to be more than my neighbor, and I'm not remotely interested."

"Let's see if we can let him really know you're not interested." Jason shoved his door open and walked around to her side to open her door. Speechless, she stayed in her seat looking up at him. "Come on, sweetheart, let's get inside." He grabbed her hand and whispered in her ear, "He's looking at us—play along."

Too surprised to resist, she allowed herself to be pulled out of the car. He shut the door behind her and put his arm around her shoulders.

As they walked onto the sidewalk, Billy approached them. "Oh, Claire, I thought someone had parked in your space and I was coming to take care of business for you." Hitching his jeans a little higher as he delivered that line, Billy then turned to look at Jason inquiringly.

Jason offered a hand and said, "Jason Danvers. Appreciate you looking out for my girlfriend, Bill."

"That's Billy or William, not Bill. I've never seen you here before. How long have you known Claire?"

"Oh we've been close for several years, isn't that right, baby?"

"Er, um, yes, several years. We usually stay at Jason's house; that's why you never see him here."

Billy's eyes darted back and forth between them as if sensing something amiss but unable to grasp exactly what it was.

"Well, Bill, it was nice meeting you. See you around, I'm sure."

As Jason led her away she heard Billy say, "It's Billy!" He took the keys from her hand and opened her apartment door, following her into the entryway. She collapsed against the wall, laughter shaking her body.

"That was so funny! You really had him torn up calling him Bill. He's very serious about his name," she managed to choke out between peals of laughter.

Jason didn't seem to see the humor in the situation that she did. "Claire, I don't know if you should take him so lightly. He seemed very territorial toward you. Are you sure that you have never had any type of relationship with him?"

"Ugh, are you kidding me? Give me credit for having some standards. I've never had any type of anything with him nor have I ever given him any hope that I would. I think he's just a lonely person who likes to imagine things are something they aren't. He probably does the same thing to all the female residents here."

With a skeptical look, he asked, "Have you ever seen him doing that?" After some thought, she reluctantly admitted that she hadn't. "Please be careful and for heaven's sake, don't do anything to encourage him. You never know about people."

Touched that he was concerned, she said, "I promise. I'll be careful. Thank you for being so concerned."

Danger, danger, look away, run, now! Even with her head telling her to run, she couldn't turn from him. Time seemed to stand still as they looked at each other.

With a muttered oath, he closed the distance between them and pulled her into his arms. "You have had me half out of my mind tonight. I've got to taste you." With that comment, Jason's lips took possession of hers. Heat slammed into her as he pulled her even closer.

She moaned as she opened her mouth to his seeking tongue. Shivers of desire and pleasure coursed through her as Jason's tongue thrust into her mouth just as his thigh pushed its way between hers. Like a starving person, she feasted on the sweet, hot stroke of his tongue. Jason's hand slid down her back to the curve of her bottom and she lost what little sense of preservation she had left by rubbing herself urgently on the erection she could feel burning against her stomach.

"Oh god, I want to be inside you, Claire. You're killing me!" With her bottom cupped in his hands, he lifted her off her feet and said roughly, "Wrap your legs around me." She wrapped her legs tightly around him, causing her dress to bunch up around her waist. His erection now pushed hotly against the thin silk of her black lace panties. His tongue blazed a trail of fire down her neck, moving closer to the swell of her aching breasts. He lowered the top of her dress, exposing the tight pebbled nipples.

She slid her hands in his soft, silky hair and moaned loudly as he took a nipple into his mouth and started to suck it. Never had she been so grateful to be without a bra. She urgently tightened her legs around him, rubbing herself harder against his erection as she felt herself close to orgasm.

"Oh God," she panted. "Oh please!"

"What do you want, baby? Tell me what you need."

"You," she croaked out. "I want you!" Almost sobbing with the force of her desire, she was helpless to stop the raging storm within her. Dimly, she heard a ringing sound. Suddenly, Suzy's voice filled the apartment from the answering machine.

She jerked back like a bucket of cold water had been dumped on her. In disbelief, she realized that she had her legs wrapped around her boss and her boss had her breast in his mouth. Despite the aching need between her legs, she started pushing at Jason and telling him to stop. He lifted his head and stared at her with flushed cheekbones and wild eyes.

"What's wrong?" he gasped out.

"We . . . we can't do this. You're my boss."

"I was your boss two minutes ago, too, and it didn't seem to matter then. What's changed exactly?" Jason asked, the frustration apparent in his strained voice.

"I . . . I lost control. I wasn't thinking. Could you please let me down?"

He reluctantly lowered his hand from her bottom, and she steadied her legs and stepped back. She quickly pulled her dress up, trying to cover her breasts again. She couldn't meet the gaze that she felt burning into her. Finally, he stepped back farther, took a few deep breaths and ran his hand raggedly through his hair. He turned to look at her again, and she saw the desire and confusion on his handsome face.

"Claire, I'm confused. I'm all for a woman's right to say no and that isn't even the main issue here. You have worked for me for what, three years now? In that time, there's never been even a close call between us romantically and then suddenly in the last week I can barely walk by you without a raging hard-on. I know that seeing you in that club over the weekend in damn near nothing probably has something to do with it, but I don't think that's the cause of what happened tonight. Who are you really, Claire, besides the person tying me up in knots? Don't even answer that," ground out Jason as he walked toward the door. "I don't think I can process anything else tonight." Without looking back, he opened her door and said, "I'll pick you up at eight in the morning. Please be ready." He shut the door quietly behind him.

She pressed her hand against her mouth as she sagged to the floor. Would sleeping with him have been any worse than the ache she was left with now? If Suzy hadn't called, they'd be in her bed or on her floor right now making love. Instead she was left with nothing but frustration and regret.

Was it regret that she let it go that far or regret that she stopped it? She didn't dare answer that question. She'd always thought Jason was drop-dead handsome and entertained many fantasies through the years concerning him, but that was as far as it went. Now, not only were some of those fantasies coming true, she was also forced to admit that she was feeling something for him other than desire, and she knew that was a huge mistake.

People like Jason didn't fall in love with people like her. She worked two jobs to take care of her mother, Louise, and herself. She couldn't afford to have an affair with her boss and lose one of those jobs. Not only would that spell disaster for her; it would also basically put her mother and Louise out of their home. She was too old for a crush. It was time to get back to the reality of being Jason's assistant and not his girlfriend or bedmate. She forced herself from the floor and made her way to the shower. She vowed that tomorrow everything would be back to a professional level. She couldn't afford for it to be otherwise.

Chapter Eleven

The next morning Claire was waiting outside her apartment at five minutes before eight and, as promised, Jason's Mercedes pulled into the parking lot at eight. Quickly opening the door before he could leave the car, she settled herself in the seat and offered a quick good morning. The morning news on the radio filled the silence in the car and offered a much-needed diversion. He seemed content to avoid all conversation, and soon they were arriving at Danvers and heading up in the elevator. Jason stepped off to get a coffee, and she continued on to their floor.

By the time Jason arrived a short time later she was hard at work replying to her e-mails from the previous day. The morning continued on as if nothing had ever happened. Around noon, he came out of his office and said, "Claire, we will need to work on Saturday and possibly Sunday this week and better plan on it for next weekend as well."

The blood drained from her face as she asked, "Why

would that be necessary? Everything is up-to-date on the merger."

"I'm going out of town for a few days to visit the headquarters for Mericom and won't return until Friday. By the time I return I'll have further revisions to make to the contract that will need to be completed by Monday. The next week will follow a similar course and there's a possibility you will need to accompany me to Grayson's, but we will finalize that next week."

"But I already have plans for those weekends!"

His steely gaze burning into hers, Jason said, "Yes, I'm sure that you do have other engagements planned. However, I feel that this job and this merger are your clear priorities and, if not, then we have a serious problem."

The threat in his voice was clear and Claire knew that if she continued, she could well find herself unemployed. "Ye . . . yes, they are, and I'll be here on Saturday. Are we starting early?" she asked hopefully.

"No, I'll be late getting in on Friday, so let's give ourselves some extra rest on Saturday and come in around lunch. We can have dinner brought in later, so no need to worry about that." With her heart sinking she managed a nod and Jason was gone. *Oh great, he isn't going to let up on the weekend work, ugh.*

She already had bachelor parties planned with Pam for the next few weeks, and they were all several hours away. She was going to have to call her and cancel and hope that Pam could find a replacement for her. She decided to put that off for later and gathered up her purse to go to the cafeteria for lunch. As luck would have it, Suzy was just coming down the hall toward her office when she stepped out. Claire walked over to the elevator where her friend was waiting.

"Hey, hey, girlfriend, I'm starving. Let's go grab some eats," Suzy said.

"Are we going to the cafeteria?"

"Nah, why don't we walk around the corner to the sandwich shop? I could use a change of scenery."

"Okay, that actually sounds good. Maybe we could get a table outside."

Suzy kept the conversation flowing until they'd reached the sandwich shop and settled into a shaded table outdoors. "So, what were all the fireworks with boss man last night?"

Nearly choking on her iced tea, Claire said, "What're you talking about?"

"Oh come on, babe, do I look like I suddenly got stupid overnight?"

She knew it was pointless to continue to act ignorant. She sighed. "I don't know, Suz. I really don't."

Suzy finally asked, "Has something been going on between you two that I don't know about?"

She decided that if she could tell anyone the whole story without being judged, it was Suzy. She poured out the story of her second job and the reasons behind it, finally coming to the part of her encounter at Jason's friend's bachelor party during the weekend and what had happened in the restroom afterwards. She kept going until she'd told Suzy everything, including what occurred the previous night. Suzy sat in silence, looking at her with her mouth opening and closing like a fish.

"Holy shit. Who are you and where is my friend Claire?" Suzy exclaimed. "I feel like I've entered the twilight zone where you turn into me, and I turn into you. Why in the world didn't you tell me what you were doing on the side? You should know that, of all people, I wouldn't give you grief about it."

Claire reached over and took her hand, seeing the hurt on her face. "I know you wouldn't, Suz. I was just embarrassed to tell anyone, including you, about my financial problems and the second job. You know I would never be doing a job like that if I didn't desperately need the money."

"Claire, we could have figured out something. I don't want you to think I would ever look down on you or judge you. Hell, I would probably do that job just for kicks."

As she leaned over to hug Suzy, she said tearfully, "No more secrets then. I'm sorry, and I know you'd never look down on me. You're not made that way."

"Okay, enough of the slobbering all over each other, tell me when you're going to do the boss man, because I'm dying to know how he is in the sack."

With a laugh, Claire playfully swatted at Suzy. "I'm not doing anything with him. It was all a mistake and he appears to regret it as much as I do."

"Yeah right. If that was regret I saw jumping between you two last night, I'll give up leather skirts and start wearing plaid."

"The lines between us got blurred with everything that happened this weekend and then with the accidental groping of him under the table last night. I think it's all going to settle back down into our normal routine now and be fine, though," she assured Suzy.

Suzy looked at her shrewdly, asking the one question she didn't have an answer for: "Do you want things to settle back to normal?"

The subject of Jason was avoided for the rest of their lunch and all too soon they were walking back to the office. Suzy asked, "Hey, you want to go out one night this week for dinner?"

"Let me see how things are with Mom and I'll let you know. I need to go by there tonight and take some groceries."

"Claire, you know that if you or your mother needs anything, you can ask me, right? I've got money saved and I would be glad to help you if you need it."

She felt like her friendship with Suzy had turned a corner since their conversation at lunch. She hugged her again and thanked her. Suzy said with her usual dramatic flair, "We're going to have to cut this hugging shit out today, or before you know it we're going to be braiding each other's hair and wearing matching pinky rings."

Laughter shaking Claire's body, she felt pounds

lighter than she had that morning with the support she'd received from Suzy.

Suddenly remembering dinner the previous night, she asked, "Hey, Suz, what did you think of Grayson? I thought I noticed some sparks flying over there as well," she joked.

"Ugh, puleeze, in his dreams! He's a stud—I'll give him that—but his blood probably actually runs blue. I've more important things to do with my time than literally have the life sucked out of me by Mr. Uptight. I mean, he probably doesn't even own a tour T-shirt—and who doesn't have a Bon-Jovi tour shirt, you know?"

"Wow, Suz, that's a lot of detailed protesting. Sounds like Mr. Uptight hit a nerve last night. I'm sure with the advent of eBay you could buy him a Bon-Jovi tour shirt." With a very rude hand gesture, Suzy stalked off toward her office and Claire laughed all the way to hers.

The rest of the week continued peacefully at work. Jason called in several times a day, but with him out of the office it was easier to believe that they could return to a normal working relationship. On Wednesday evening she'd splurged and took her mother and Louise for dinner. Her mother didn't like going out much anymore. She preferred having her meal while watching her favorite TV shows. Luckily, she was having a good day, and Claire enjoyed the time with her.

The one unpleasant aspect of the week had been

calling Pam to cancel for the weekend and also inform-
ing her that she would not be able to work the next
weekend as well. To say Pam was upset was an understatement. Livid was a more accurate word. Pam had
informed her that she would be hiring someone and,
rather than her normal assurance that Claire could
work all the weekend parties, it would now be a matter
of who Pam felt more comfortable scheduling.

Claire had a feeling that her employment with Partiez Plus would be ending soon. The overtime pay for
the weekend work from Danvers would be sufficient to
fill the gap until she could find another weekend job. It
was possible she might have to work several part-time
jobs to compensate for the loss of income but, as usual,
she would do what needed to be done.

She had promised to have a drink with Suzy after
work on Friday night, and she was looking forward to
hanging out with her. Just as she was finishing up for
the day, Suzy glided into her office. "Hey, chick, you
ready to split?"

"Yep, just finishing up here." Grimacing down at her
tan slacks and equally plain white blouse, she added,
"I wish I had on something a little less. . . ."

"Drab, dull, old lady?" Suzy added helpfully.

With a swat to her friend's arm, she said, "I was going to say formal, but thank you for those kind words."
Suzy of course could never be called any of those
things. Today, while wearing a black leather miniskirt
with fishnet stockings, mile-high heels, and a hot-pink

T-shirt with a skull on it, she was as far removed from boring as you could possibly get.

Claire locked up and soon they were on their way to a bar a few blocks away where Suzy liked to hang out. Claire had never been to this particular place, and she dearly hoped it wasn't some type of biker bar. Suzy was blessed to fit in wherever she went; unfortunately, the same wasn't true for her.

With a quick prayer of thanks, she was relieved to see that the bar was actually upscale, with what looked to be mainly professionals having a drink after work. They grabbed a couple of seats at the bar as Suzy yelled, "Hey, our phone numbers for anyone who buys us a drink."

Horrified, she said, "Suz, are you crazy?"

By the time she finished her sentence, there were six drinks sitting in front of them. "I haven't bought a drink in years—why would I start tonight? Don't sweat it; we will give them fake numbers, unless they're really hot."

Claire picked up the drink that looked the most harmless. It was sweet and tasted of pineapple and strawberry. "You better watch yourself; that baby will knock you on your ass," Suzy advised.

"It doesn't taste like alcohol. I think it's safer than those shots." Halfway through the first drink, two men approached them and took credit for a couple of the drinks. She was surprised to find that she could relax and enjoy flirting and making conversation.

The men, Chris and Joe, were surprisingly easy to talk to, and having them sit beside the girls discouraged other men from approaching Suzy for the phone-number payout she'd promised. She realized after the first drink that Suzy was right. It might look harmless, but her head was already spinning. Chris and Joe teased her about switching to iced tea, but she told them she had to drive home and couldn't afford to be facedown somewhere along the way.

Around ten, she told Suzy she was tired and was ready to leave. Much to her surprise, Suzy insisted on leaving as well. When they stepped outside, she said, "Suz, you didn't have to leave. You were having fun. Go back in for a while."

"Nah, I'm dragging, and I was getting ready to bail anyway."

"Are you sure? You looked like you were really enjoying Chris."

"That was just a drink you, nothing else."

Confused, she asked, "A 'drink you'?"

"Yeah, instead of 'thank you,' when someone buys you a drink and you chat them up afterward it's a drink you."

"Um, okay, that must be Suzy language. I've never heard of it," she said and laughed. "Sorry I needed to leave early. I just wanted to have a good night's sleep before working this weekend."

"Oh, that's right; you and Hot Buns are working. Why, I wonder, are you suddenly working weekends when you never have before?"

"It's because of the merger with Mericom."

"You mean stuffed shirt Gray is so uptight that you guys have to work seven days a week to keep up with his demands?" Suzy sneered.

"Suz, I don't think it's that. It's just the extra time being spent on that project is causing Jason's other work to fall behind. I'm sure Grayson isn't as bad as you make him out to be."

"Yeah, right. The man needs to learn how to loosen up. I bet he doesn't even own a pair of boxers; briefs all the way, no doubt."

"Um, sweetie, how did we get on the subject of Grayson's underwear choices? It seems to be that you have a very suspect amount of interest in Grayson," Claire teased.

Suzy stalked ahead of her and grumbled over her shoulder, "I was just making an observation. No need to get your panties in a wad." Claire ran to catch up with her, giving her a brief hug as they walked on.

Claire scanned the area and saw no sign of Billy. She was almost to her front door when she heard a voice behind her and looked around to find that Billy had indeed seen her arrive. "Hey, Claire, where's your boyfriend tonight?" Billy asked in a sullen tone.

"Er. . . . he's out of town tonight. He should be back soon, though."

"How come you never mentioned you were dating anyone?"

She was starting to get angry as well at the nasty tone in his voice. "Billy, I really think my private life is my business, don't you?" Billy's face reddened as she stuck her key in her lock and quickly opened her door.

Before she could close it, Billy said, "I thought you were different. I guess I was wrong." Not bothering to reply, she slammed her door shut and vowed that she would start looking for another place to live. It was obvious that Billy was going to continue to be a problem.

She didn't think the idea of her having a boyfriend would help, especially since said boyfriend wasn't likely to be at her place again. *Great, like my life isn't hectic enough, now I've a nut-job neighbor stalking me.* The confrontation with Billy took some of the enjoyment out of the evening. After a quick shower, she climbed into bed and tried to forget the angry expression on Billy's face. Maybe Jason was right about him after all.

Chapter Twelve

Saturday morning she was up and out early. She picked up a few things at the market that Louise had requested, then dropped them by, along with her mother's medicine, and spent an enjoyable hour eating breakfast and chatting. Her mother was having another good day, and seeing how well she was doing this week made Claire that much more determined to keep her mother in her home no matter what it took.

All too soon it was time to go to the office. It felt strange to see the usually full parking garage bare but for a few other cars. The office door was ajar when she arrived on their floor, and Jason was already seated at his desk with his door open. She stored her handbag and walked through his door to see what he needed her to work on. He leaned back in his leather chair and studied her as she approached his desk.

"Thanks for coming in today. I hope it didn't interfere with your weekend plans." The amused smirk on his face told her exactly what plans he was referring to.

"No, not at all. What should I get started on?"

Completely ignoring her question, Jason continued on. "No big party this weekend, huh?"

"Did we come here to work or to discuss my private life?"

"Well, if your private life is open for discussion, I would be happy to put work aside, because, quite frankly, I'm dying to hear more about your other life as a stripper."

Claire could only look at him in surprise. Since he hadn't broached the subject of her second job during the week, she assumed he had decided to let it go. The look on his face assured her that he had far from forgotten it and intended to have that discussion now. "I don't think my private life is any of your business, so, no, it isn't open for discussion," she snapped.

"Oh, that's where you're wrong. It is indeed my business when it reflects on Danvers. Now have a seat and let's have this long-overdue discussion, shall we?"

What the hell am I doing? I had no intention of having this conversation today. She'd reduced him to an aching, obsessing mess in the last week. That night in her apartment, with her wrapped around him, still haunted him so much he could barely concentrate on what was the biggest deal this company had ever been involved in. This was about the worst time possible to go crazy over a woman. That never happened. He enjoyed women but always on his own terms. Never had someone so completely confused and intrigued him.

The one piece to the puzzle that he couldn't figure out was the side job. Sure, people worked two jobs all the time—hell he felt like he worked three most of the time—so that wasn't the confusing part. It was the second job that she'd obviously chosen that floored him. She was about as far from a stripper as he could imagine. Okay, so she didn't actually take all her clothes off, but she was damn near naked when she popped out of that cake. She was beautiful, and no doubt men loved looking at her. He hated to admit that. He had never noticed exactly how beautiful she was until the weekend with Liz and Harold.

She presented a whole different person daily in the office and, even though Jason was sure he had noticed she was attractive, he had never been tempted to cross the line with her. Now he was practically running and clawing his way across that line. She'd become an ache that he couldn't get past. He needed to have her, be inside her, but more than that, he needed to know what was going on with her because none of it made any sense to him.

He rarely thought or cared what was going on in any woman's life he was seeing. His life was this company and that left very little to give to anyone else. With Claire, though, it was fast becoming her first and the company second. It had to just be the mystery there.

Once he had his questions answered then life could return to normal.

She seated herself stiffly in the chair in front of Jason, and the silence stretched as he seemed to be lost in thought. "Jason?"

His name seemed to jerk him back to the present, and he said, "Um . . . yes, where were we?"

Confused, she said, "You wanted to tell me why my private life was your business, I believe."

"Oh, yes, let's see. . . . Why don't we just start at the beginning? How long have you been working your, er . . . second job?"

Stiffly, she replied, "About a year."

Jason looked at her in surprise. "You have been stripping for a year and I never knew it?"

"It's not stripping and you know that," she defended hotly.

"Okay, okay, I mean cake jumping or whatever you call it. Claire, truthfully, I'm a little baffled here. No offense to her, but Suzy I could easily see doing that. You, not so much. Suzy is a very secure person who wants and enjoys the attention of men, and it shows. That's her personality; it's who she is and that's great. You, however, obviously don't want or seek that type of attention. If you did, your main wardrobe color wouldn't be tan or brown, and I'm quite sure I would have seen a hint of cleavage before. Well, other than in the last week. I know you didn't just decide you needed some excitement. So, what gives, Claire?"

*   *   *

As she studied Jason, her first reaction was to tell him to go to hell and that it was none of his business. If anything that he said had held one hint of sarcasm, she would have done just that. But he seemed genuinely concerned and confused. With a deep breath, she started all the way back with the death of her father and sister and continued on to her mother's health problems and the financial strain of maintaining her house, buying her medication, and the reason why she couldn't live with her.

Once the words started pouring out of her, she didn't even realize that she had tears running down her face until she felt one drop on her hand. He leaned quietly over the desk and handed her some tissues. She turned to the side to dry her face before looking at him. Terrified that he would be looking at her with disgust or pity, she was surprised to see admiration in his eyes. "Claire, I'd no idea," he said quietly. "Why didn't you tell me what was going on?"

"Why would I? You're my employer. It's not your job to handle the personal problems of your employees."

"Claire, I would think you'd know me well enough by now to see that I'm not a bottom-line employer. I do care about every single person who works here. This company wouldn't be where it is without you and the other employees. I would never turn my back on anyone in trouble."

Her eyes started to well up again as tears threatened. "I do know that, Jason, but I've never had any-one to depend on and truthfully this is more than a little embarrassing for me. I've managed to get by. If I need to work five jobs to make ends meet, then I will. I have to."

He settled back in his chair and said, "Claire, let me help you. Danvers does extensive work in this com-munity, and I would be happy to know some of that work would benefit someone whom I . . . er . . . Dan-vers values so highly. If you furnish me with the cost of all of your mother's medication, I'll see that you have a check by Monday. Furthermore, we have a construc-tion crew on our payroll as well. They'll be sent to your mother's home on Monday to make all the repairs that are needed."

She jumped to her feet, anger sweeping through her, and yelled, "I'm not your charity case, Jason! I can take care of myself!"

"This isn't charity. It's assistance I would offer it to any of my employees."

"So let me get this straight—if Mona the janitor needed financial assistance, you'd offer to take care of all of her expenses? Oh, wait—does it have to be some-one you want to sleep with or is anyone eligible?"

Color darkened Jason's cheeks, and she could see the anger burning in his eyes. "I think you have made your opinion of me perfectly clear. Now unless you have any other derogatory remarks to make about my character, I would like to get to work," Jason said icily.

He handed her a folder across the desk. "Please make the changes I've indicated." She remained in front of his desk. He lifted his brow and said, "That will be all. Please close my door on the way out."

She shut the door behind her and sat down at her desk. Putting her face in her hands, she wondered why she didn't feel better about defending herself. He had seriously looked wounded at her refusal to accept his offer. Maybe he expected the poor working people here to drop to their knees in gratitude if the mighty Jason Danvers offered them something. Well, she wouldn't be some charity case to appease his rich conscience.

The day passed by quietly, with Jason's door remaining firmly closed. Dinner was delivered around six from a local deli and Claire took Jason his sandwich. Without looking up at her, he pointed to the corner of his desk and said curtly, "Just leave it there." She quietly shut the door behind her and tried to choke down her sandwich past the lump in her throat.

He had e-mailed her some additional work that he needed completed and at eight he opened his door and asked her if she was ready to go. She grabbed her purse and walked toward the door. "I'll see you to your car unless that much of my company would offend you in any way." She remained quiet and soon they were approaching her car. As she unlocked her door, she asked him what time they'd be working on Sunday.

"I've had something come up that I need to attend

to on Sunday, so we will continue work on Monday. I'm sure you could use the time from . . . the office." She knew he had really meant she could use the time away from him. Even though he had left her on her own all day, the office had vibrated with tension.

It was quite apparent that he was furious with her. Did he think she would fall on her knees before him and weep with gratitude? Maybe she could have phrased her refusal more politely. He'd blindsided her with his offer and she'd reacted on pure instinct. She couldn't help but think that his offer was more of an advance payment for sex rather than a real need to help her.

She spotted Billy as soon as she opened her door. She was so not in the mood for him tonight. She'd put Jason in his place today. Maybe it was time to do the same with Billy. With a slam of her door, she whirled around to face him. "Claire . . . I . . . I'm sorry for bothering you, and you don't have to worry about it anymore." She couldn't have been more stunned if he had opened his mouth and started barking. He continued. "I know you don't really want to go to the Neil Diamond show with Billy, and that's cool. I hope things go good with your boyfriend and if anyone here gives you any problem, you just let old Billy know, okay?" Too stunned to do more than nod, she watched him walk away.

Could this day get any stranger? First her boss offers to essentially be her fairy godmother, and now her stalker neighbor volunteers to stop stalking her and protect her from other stalkers as well. Weird. At least her day could end on some kind of positive note. Going inside, she hoped she could get a good night's sleep and that she could forget the look on Jason's face.

Chapter Thirteen

A good night's sleep seemed to be too much to hope for. Claire had tossed and turned all night, and even though she knew she'd been right to turn down Jason's offer, it still went against her nature to talk to someone the way she had to Jason. Other than being mad that he hadn't forced her into bed with him, he had probably washed the whole incident from his mind already. She, however, would never be free of the memory.

She grabbed a quick shower and got ready to go to her mother's house. She usually went through her mother's bills a few times a month, which was a chore that she dreaded. Not that she minded helping, and if there was sufficient money to pay everything it would be a breeze. Instead, she was forced to spend several hours deciding which bills had priority and which could be put off until the next month.

Louise gave her a quick hug when she walked to the study to get started. Her mother always took her nap at this time of the morning so it was quiet and easier to concentrate. Louise left an estimate on the desk from her nephew on repairing the roof damage. He had written a note that the roof needed replacing, which would cost approximately $20,000, and to make repairs that he didn't feel would last through the winter would cost $5,000.

She laid her head down on the desk. There was no way she could cover the cost of the patch, much less replacing the roof. Even with income from several jobs it would take some time to save that much money and, apparently, time was something in short supply with the current state of the roof. She would talk to the credit union at work on Monday and see if she could work out a loan to at least cover the repairs. It would hopefully buy her several months to decide what she was going to do. The additional monthly payment of a loan would be hard to make, but what choice did she have?

The rest of the stack was just as depressing. Dividing up the money that was left after living expenses, she made a small payment against almost all the medical bills. She didn't know how much longer they could keep going. Her finances were built on a stack of cards and sooner or later the cards always folded. Until they did, she would keep hoping for a miracle every day. *You turned down your miracle yesterday. It's not likely to come along twice.*

Maybe she should have accepted Jason's offer after all. Was jumping out of a cake nearly nude actually less damaging to her pride than taking charity? If it was just the charity part, it would be easier to accept; it was the part of feeling like he would expect something in bed as repayment that was harder to handle. He'd never given her a reason to think that, but then things had never been anything but professional between them.

She knew the taste of his tongue now, the curve of his face, the feel of his erection pressing against her. When she closed her eyes she could almost feel him against her, his breath on her neck, his hands stroking down her back and over her hips. She tried to shake the memories of her daydream from her mind. She gave herself an extra few minutes before she joined her mother and Louise for lunch.

Her mother was confused today. She called her Chrissie the entire time and any attempts to correct her only led to agitation. It was so disappointing because she'd seemed better the last few visits. Today, she was quite obviously hovering close to the edge. Claire finally decided to take her leave rather than to continue to upset her mom. Louise looked at her sympathetically and walked her to the door as usual.

"It happens sometimes, honey. She just comes and goes. Now you go on home and get you some rest and don't worry about anything else today."

As her eyes began to well up, she pulled Louise into a hug and said, "Oh, Louise, I love you."

"I love you too. Now go on and get yourself home. We will be just fine here."

She waved at her until she was out of sight. Some

rest today did sound good, she was sure she would need it for the upcoming week. Idly, she wondered what Jason was doing and then chastised herself for even caring. He was her boss. That was all she ever needed to know about him. Even as she tried to convince herself of that, she knew it was a lie.

Monday morning arrived and Claire was in the rush hour traffic before she knew it. She was glad to see when she arrived at the office that Jason wasn't in yet. Suzy called to ask her to lunch later and she happily accepted. Maybe this would be a good day after all. She was so engrossed in her work, she'd not noticed the door opening and was surprised to look up and see Jason staring at her.

"Good morning, Claire. You look happy today."

"Oh, good morning. I didn't hear you come in."

"So, why are you so happy today—anything special?"

"No, not really." Claire turned back toward her computer and hoped that he would continue into his office.

"You look pretty today," Jason said as he walked into his office and shut the door.

She looked at his retreating figure in shock. Had he really just said she looked pretty? Surely she'd misunderstood. He seemed to have put their argument behind him, and she felt she could do no less.

Around midmorning, she remembered to call the credit union concerning her loan. She was surprised and delighted to hear that they could take her application over the telephone. Within a few moments, her application was approved, and she was asked to stop by and pick up her check at the end of the day.

Just as she was ending the call, Leslie, the creditor, explained that they were running a special promotion and that she qualified to defer her first payment for six months with no interest or fees. She almost wept with happiness as she assured Leslie that she would love to take advantage of the offer. She ended the call and twirled in her chair in happiness.

Finally, she was getting a break and it felt great. At the end of her second twirl, she faced her boss. "Er . . . sorry about that. Just taking a short break."

With a laugh, Jason said, "I can see that. Please keep going. It's good to see you enjoying yourself."

Self-consciously, she straightened in her seat and tried to return her expression back to professionalism. "Was there something you needed me for?"

Smiling at her, Jason replied, "Yes, I wanted to go over this weekend with you. Grayson has decided to travel here and stay at my home, so we will be working from there. I would like for you to come over Saturday morning and be prepared to stay until Sunday afternoon." Then, looking uncomfortable, he continued. "Um . . . Grayson asked if Suzy might be free to come as well. This isn't a working weekend for her, and I'm not insisting that she come. This is purely her choice, and I've no problem with whatever she decides."

"Does Grayson like Suzy?"

Jason replied, looking uncomfortable, "I think she's different and that intrigues him. Again, please let Suzy know that I'm not requesting she come along; this is totally up to her. Of course, knowing Suzy, she won't have a problem telling me no, regardless." Jason laughed.

Claire chuckled. "You're right about that. Are you going to be back in today?"

"Why? Are you going to miss me if I'm not?" Unable to resist this teasing side of Jason, she laughed and assured him that she would be just fine. "Actually, I've a lunch meeting that will run into the afternoon. I probably won't see you again until tomorrow morning."

With a warm smile, he left before she could reply. She tried to assure herself that she was just feeling so happy because everything had worked out well with her loan. She was still smiling when she collected her purse and locked up to meet Suzy for lunch.

Chapter Fourteen

They'd decided to go to the outdoor café around the corner again and Suzy was waiting for her in the lobby. Today she was dressed in a denim skirt—short, of course. Suzy's tanned bare legs appeared to sparkle from some type of glitter. Mile-high red platform sandals that wrapped several inches up her legs and a red silk tank top with a black vest completed her look. Claire was sure Suzy's boss was relieved to see a shirt with no writing or advertisements on it.

Suzy talked about her weekend as they found a table and placed their order. After taking a long drink of her iced tea, Suzy asked, "So, how are things with Hot Buns? Any more bumping and grinding?" Wiggling her eyebrows suggestively, Suzy laughed as her face turned bright red.

"You're horrible. Why do I tell you anything?"

"Maybe because you need my fresh insight into your dull-but-not-yet-hopeless sex life?"

"There's nothing new to tell—well, nothing of the

bumping variety, at least. Jason and I did have sort of an argument last week, though."

"Do tell. Was it at least over sex?" Suzy asked hopefully.

"No, get your mind out of the gutter. Everything doesn't resolve around sex."

"Well, why the hell not?"

"It was over money and maybe I made it into something about sex," she admitted.

As the waiter delivered their lunch Suzy impatiently shooed him away and said, "Get on with it!"

"Well, he asked me to explain my, er . . . weekend job to him, and when I told him I needed the money, he wanted to know why. I told him about my mother, her medical bills, and the upkeep on her house. I basically poured the whole thing out and then he starts barking off instructions. He wanted me to get him the amount of my mother's medication for the month and to give him the address of my mother's home so he could line up the construction crew from Danvers to make all the necessary repairs. He told me he would have a check waiting for me today. I just went off on him, Suzy. I was so mad at him for wanting to make me his charity case or, worse yet, wanting to buy his way into my bed. Can you believe him? I also told him I felt sure he wouldn't be making the same offer to Mona the janitor if she were in my position!"

Finished, she waited for the approval that she knew would be coming and was surprised when Suzy instead gave her an almost pitying look.

"Oh, babe, I'm all for sticking it to someone when they deserve it but if you were going to throw something back in Mr. D.'s face, you should have picked something better than money. The man seems to give it out hand-over-fist and, trust me, it's got nothing to do with sex. You know Cindy who works in my department?" Claire nodded her head as she pictured the little dynamo with a personality much like Suzy's. "Remember last year when she was knocked up? Well, her husband lost his job when she was getting close to popping and somehow Jason found out about it. He actually went to her house one evening and talked to her so that she wouldn't be embarrassed at the office. He paid their bills for two months until she had her baby and her husband was employed again. He said he didn't want the stress to cause problems with her pregnancy. She said he was so sweet, and she cried all over him. Oh, and George, when his girlfriend had the surgery thingy a few months back, said Jason stopped by the hospital to visit and offered to pay the difference left after her insurance. I'm sure they're both good-looking chicks, but I don't think he wants to get them in the sack—you know what I'm saying?"

Claire was stunned. How could she work so closely with him and never know about any of this? Wouldn't someone in his position want the credit for so many good deeds? She felt horrible, remembering all the nasty things she'd said to him. He hadn't wanted to help her for sex; actually it was embarrassing to assume that a man like him would need to buy sex from someone like her. After he got over his anger, he probably had a big laugh over that.

God, was there ever a time that she'd been this embarrassed? With a groan, she put her hands over her face and felt Suzy reach over and pat her on the back. "It's okay, babe. We all make an ass out of ourselves from time to time. You have just done it a little more than usual lately."

"Um . . . thanks for that, Suz," she said weakly. "I have to apologize to him, but how exactly do I do that?"

"Well, let's see," Suzy began helpfully. " 'Hey, Hot Buns. Sorry I threw your offer back in your face. I just wanted you to know that I would be glad to give it up for free. You don't have to offend me by trying to pay for it.' "

"Oh, thanks! I'm sure that would sound so much better, and I don't want to give it up for free."

"So you do want to be paid, after all?" Suzy said, wiggling her brows.

"No, you pervert. I don't want to give it up at all, as you so nicely put it. Speaking of giving it up, though, Jason wanted me to ask if you'd like to come to his house this weekend. We're working there with Grayson on the merger and apparently Grayson asked if you'd come as well."

"Ugh . . . really? That stuffed shirt thinks he's going to get his groove on with me? I mean, he's good-looking and all, but it's a damn shame he's such a tight ass. He probably thinks I'm some call girl he can buy for the weekend to rock his little uptight world. Nope, I don't see it happening for him. Tell Jason I'd rather pick lint out of my belly button." Suzy seemed to protest a little too much every time the subject of Grayson was brought up.

Although maybe someone like Grayson was exactly what Suzy needed after the heartache that Jeff had caused. She put on a really brave face, but she knew that Suzy was still hurting inside and the front that she presented was really to protect her heart. "I might not be interested in going, but I'm really interested in what you plan to do there."

"I'm going there to work, nothing more."

"Mm-hmm, is that what they call it these days?"

"It's not like that and we won't be alone. Grayson will be there and probably others as well. It's strictly professional, so get your mind out of the gutter."

With a sly look, Suzy said, "We will see, girlie. You forget I saw you two at dinner last week, and the looks between you were actually making *my* underwear melt. I can't imagine you being under the same roof and being able to control yourself. Just rip each other's clothes off and see where it goes from there. I do insist on details though as soon as you get home. Call me, text me, e-mail me . . . just get me the four-one-one on exactly what happened."

With a laugh, Claire moved the conversation to safer subjects and thoroughly enjoyed her lunch.

*   *   *

The next day, Claire was in the office before Jason arrived and used the extra time to arrange for the repairs to her mother's home. She'd picked up the check from the credit union the day before and was still overjoyed at how simple the process had been.

When he arrived a short time later, she greeted him with a smile and a cheerful "good morning." As if almost surprised, he returned the greeting and stopped in front of her desk.

He looked at her warmly and asked, "How are you today?"

"Very good, thanks."

"I'm going to be out of the office for most of today, but I wondered if you were free for dinner tonight."

Surprised, she replied, "Dinner?"

At her obvious confusion, Jason quickly added, "It's really a business dinner. I'll be out of the office for the rest of the week at Mericom in Charleston, and I want to go over a few things with you before I leave. Since we both have to eat, I thought dinner would work out well."

"I can stay late and we could go over everything here when you get back, if you'd prefer."

"That's not necessary. We can eat somewhere close to your apartment. How about the Italian place that's down the street from you, Villa Risso?"

"They have great food, but it's very casual, if that's a problem," she added.

"No, I like casual. Let's say around seven. Does that give you enough time?" She agreed and after picking up some files from his office, he left with a quick good-bye.

The afternoon passed quickly in nervous anticipation. She kept trying to remind herself that this was a business dinner and not a date. There was no reason to be nervous. She left promptly at five so that she would have time to go home and freshen up before meeting Jason. Luckily, she didn't run into Suzy on her way out. She could just imagine what type of graphic comments she would have made.

Chapter Fifteen

Claire went straight to the shower when she arrived home. After getting out, she threw on her robe and walked over to the vanity to touch up her makeup. As she was leaning over the vanity to apply her blush, the sleeve of her robe caught the small wooden box that she used to store her toiletries and it came crashing off and landed painfully hard on her right foot. *Shit! Owwww! God, that hurts!*

She hobbled to her bed to assess the damage. Her big toe was now bleeding profusely. She grabbed some tissue and held it against her toe until it looked as if the blood flow was slowing. Upon inspection, she was dismayed to see that her toenail had been cut. She hobbled back to the bathroom for her trusty first aid box and located a Band-Aid and antiseptic spray. Soon, she had an ugly—but functional—white bandage around her toe. With a sigh, she thought she should really start avoiding the bathroom since most of her accidents seemed to occur there.

She had planned to wear a long blue sundress she'd purchased on a whim several years ago and a pair of flat, white sandals. The dress might still be possible. The shoes, however, weren't, since the toe openings were too small for the bandage. Almost ready to admit defeat, she spotted a pair of flip-flops she kept to wear on the beach. After sliding on her dress, she gingerly tried on the flip-flops. It wasn't as bad as she'd feared.

The shoes gave the dress a more casual appearance, and of course there was no missing the huge bandage on her toe, but from the ankles up she looked fine. If she could arrive at the restaurant first and be seated before Jason, he might never notice her toe. After quickly finishing her makeup and locking up her apartment, she made her way to her car. *Oh great, instead of looking sexy, I'm waddling like a duck.*

The restaurant was only a few minutes from her apartment and she arrived fifteen minutes early. The parking lot was already crowded and Claire was forced to park almost at the end of the lot. Walking so far was going to be painful and she grimaced as she got out of her car and locked her door. She was so intent on making her way to the front of the restaurant as gently as possible that she didn't notice another car entering the lot. She jumped as she felt a hand cup her elbow. "Owwww! Ouch!"

Jason peered down at her foot in concern. "I'm sorry I startled you. I thought you heard me. What happened?"

"I knocked something on my foot and the toenail is . . . Well, you don't want to hear the details, but I hurt my toe."

Looking down at her injury, he asked, "Do you need to go to the hospital?"

"No, it will be fine. It's just a little sore now."

"Would you rather I just take you home? I can't stand the thought of causing you further pain."

She looked up into Jason's beautiful blue eyes, so filled with concern for her ,and knew that she would not give up this time with him for anything, even a little toe pain. "It's fine, really; it already feels better."

He continued to study her for a few moments and then tightened his arm around her. "Lean on me and let's walk slowly. Let me know if you need to stop." Maybe it was his nearness and the feel of his arm holding her close, but she didn't feel any pain as they made their way into the restaurant.

Jason walked up to the host and smiled. "Carlo, it's so good to see you again."

"Mr. Danvers, what a pleasure, and you brought such a beautiful companion tonight. I have the perfect table. It has a lot of privacy for you and your lady."

Not bothering to correct him, Jason said a sincere thank-you, and they were led to a secluded table in the corner. She was grateful when Jason pulled out a chair for her and carefully assisted her into the seat. After he was seated he asked her if she had any preferences in wine, but she was happy to leave the decision to him.

Soon Carlo had departed, leaving their menus and promising to return with the wine that Jason had selected.

"Are you doing okay, Claire?"

"I'm fine, really. Thanks."

"Let me know if you're feeling any discomfort. Would you like a chair to elevate your foot?"

"Er . . . no, that's okay." She could just imagine her bandaged foot complete with flip-flop sticking out in a chair for Jason and the other customers to see. That was not going to happen.

Carlo returned with their wine and poured them both a glass before taking their orders. She decided on a simple meal of lasagna, and surprisingly Jason indicated that he would have the same. "You must come here often if they know you by name."

"I usually dine here at least once a week. I love Italian food."

"Is this on your way home, then?"

"I've got a house on the ocean about fifteen minutes from here depending on traffic, and I admit to eating a certain amount of takeout during the week." Jason laughed

She was pleasantly surprised that he seemed so normal. He was no doubt a millionaire, yet talking with him like this, you'd never know that. Most people in his position would have a cook or someone responsible for taking care of the details of his life, such as his meals, but he seemed to be completely self-sufficient. Even at the office he never expected to be waited on. He went to the cafeteria for his own food or coffee, and didn't ask her to run any type of personal errands for him.

Of course she knew that he was wealthy, but there was never actually anything flashy that reminded her of that fact. Well, maybe the Mercedes. Somehow, that made her respect him even more. After working for him for three years, she still felt like she'd never really known Jason the man. With Suzy's revelations about his generosity, she was more intrigued than she would care to admit. How could someone as accomplished and powerful as Jason also be the man sitting across the table in a quiet, low-key Italian restaurant?

Jason the tycoon and object of various fantasies over the years was safe. The Jason she'd gotten to know over the last few weeks was oh-so-dangerous to her. This was a man to whom she could lose her head and her heart if she wasn't careful. Or was it already too late to save herself? And did she even want to anymore?

She noticed him studying her intently and felt her cheeks flush. "You look beautiful tonight, Claire. Blue suits you."

"Thanks. You look beautiful too. I . . . I mean, you look nice," she stammered. *Oh great, I'm treating a business dinner like my senior prom, and I just told my boss that he looked beautiful. Please, table, open up and swallow me now.*

With a grin, Jason replied, "I liked the beautiful comment best."

Embarrassed, she asked, "What did you want to go over tonight?" She reached for her purse and pulled out a small notebook and pen, then looked at him expectantly.

"Let's wait on business until after dinner, shall we? It's been a very long day and I could use some time to relax, if that's okay." She studied him, noticing the signs of fatigue around his eyes. He always made everything seem so effortless and his energy seemed to be limitless. But maybe this merger was starting to wear on him. She'd no doubt he was putting in more hours in the evening after he left the office than anyone was aware.

Tenderness flickered in her chest as she gently said, "That sounds great. I know you must be tired."

"You have no idea. I love nothing better than putting a deal together, but this particular one has come close to consuming my life. I look forward to a much-needed break after this closes."

"When do you think that will be?"

"Within the next few months, barring any other last-minute issues."

"That reminds me," she began. "I asked Suzy about this weekend and she . . . already has plans."

Jason smiled as he picked up on the hesitation in her voice and said, "Told you no way, huh?"

A laugh sputtered out of her as she said, "You really do know Suzy well, don't you?"

"Yes, and I'm betting her answer was a bit more graphic than you're letting on."

"After her recent breakup, I don't think she's ready to get back out there again yet." *Plus, she thinks Grayson is a tight ass and not in a good way.*

"Grayson does seem very interested in her," Jason said. "He's a good guy and will be in the office quite a lot after the merger."

With a smile, she said, "He seems a little . . . normal for her, so I'm not sure anything would ever come of it."

"Well stranger things have happened, so let's leave it to fate, shall we?" The waiter delivered their lasagna and a basket of fresh bread, and soon they were both enjoying their meal and Claire was finding it harder to remember this wasn't a date.

Jason looked across the table at Claire as she laughed and picked the fork up from her lap. Mishaps did seem to follow her wherever she went. First, she'd arrived for dinner with her toe bandaged and was in pain hobbling toward the door and now, when gesturing with her fork while talking, she'd somehow flipped it from her hands and up in the air with it finally landing in her lap.

She called it bad fortune; he called it endearing. It was obvious she was quite used to the frequent mishaps and had learned how to handle them with grace through the years. *God, she looks so beautiful and sexy tonight.* He had seldom seen her wear anything with color in it, and the blue dress she was wearing seemed to make her sparkle. Her eyes were luminous. Her tanned shoulders had felt smooth and soft when he had put his arm around them to help her inside earlier. Her scent was intoxicating and he was again grateful for a tablecloth covering his groin.

This whole dinner thing was probably a mistake. The idea had just popped into his head this morning when he had seen her sitting there at her desk, smiling up at him with those beautiful soft lips. Before he knew it, the invitation had been issued. He was damn lucky he hadn't already blown this merger by now. If they could just get the sex out of the way, he would be able to breathe again, to focus. They were both adults, so when whatever it was between them burned out, life could return to normal. He could be in public without having a constant erection and business would again be foremost in his mind.

He was so damn angry when she'd thrown his offer of financial assistance back in his face with the insulting accusation that he needed to buy sex. Someone being willing had never been an issue for him. He kept his affairs out of the office and off the front page. The women he had been involved with through the years knew exactly where they stood with him. They enjoyed each other while it lasted, but they always came second to the company.

His mother was constantly harping on him to settle down. No doubt because she felt it was expected and his answer to that was: Why? When he came to the point in his life where he was content and no longer felt driven to complete the next big deal, then he might entertain the thought. Something in his chest tightened when he looked at Claire and thought of her settling down with someone else in the future.

At least he'd found a way to help her without offending her again. If she ever found out, there would probably be hell to pay, but right now it seemed worth it to see the happy, relaxed expression on her face. Hopefully not having to worry about finances or her neighbor for a while would make her life easier. Soon, he would get her out of his system and his life would be his own again. And he would insist that she benefit enough to do away with the weekend job permanently.

Claire ruefully pulled the fork from her lap and laughed. "At least I didn't stab myself with it." Dinner had been wonderful, full of laughter and shared stories. Jason seemed interested in every boring detail of her life up until the present. She mainly talked about her mother and Chrissie. In turn, he told of his summers growing up around the beach with an often absent mother, who tended to drink too much and needed to be taken care of, and a workaholic father.

He said he probably didn't have any siblings because they simply forgot to take care of it as they did most everything other than Danvers. Luckily his mother's sister, Ella, had lived with them and tried to provide him with some type of maternal figure. It was obvious from the warm tone of his voice that he loved her very much. Ella had since moved to Florida and lived in a retirement community that Claire suspected Jason paid for.

His parents lived in Charleston, where his mother, to keep up appearances, chaired several charities. His father golfed most every day and still attended the occasional board meeting at Danvers. His childhood that she thought would be so vastly different from her own held many similarities. She could tell that, for the most part, he had never been a child. He seemed to always be taking care of either his mother or Ella. The neglect of his childhood, Claire thought, still seemed preferable to the abuse of hers.

Looking at her watch, she was surprised to see that two hours had passed. They'd long finished dinner and dessert and were now just drinking coffee and talking. "Oh wow, it's getting late," she said, picking up her pen and pad again. "We had better go over what you need for the rest of the week."

"You know what?" Jason asked. "I really don't want to ruin a great evening talking about business. This is the most relaxing meal I've had in weeks and I just want to leave it at that."

"Sure, you can call or e-mail me tomorrow." The waiter returned and Jason settled the check. Carefully putting his arm around her again, he helped her back to her car.

"Are you okay to drive with that foot?"

"I'm fine, really. It looks a lot worse than it is."

Jason made no move to remove his arm from her shoulders and finally she started to pull away from him. He turned her to face him in his arms and lowered his mouth to hers. She was too surprised to resist as she felt the warm touch of his soft lips meet hers, lightly at first, nibbling and tracing the outer curve of her lips almost questioningly. With a groan, she parted her lips and he swooped in to take advantage, thrusting his tongue inside to mate with hers.

Jason pulled her body closer. His hands molded her curves to fit his. She could feel his arousal pressing against her belly. As he slid his lips down the side of her neck, he whispered in her ear, "Claire, God, I want you so much. Go home with me tonight?" He pressed her hand to the front of his slacks, letting her feel the force of his desire.

As her knees started to buckle against him, she looped her arms around his neck and said, "My place . . . it's right down the street . . . please." He raised his head to look into her eyes, and whatever he saw there seemed to give him the answer he was seeking.

Jason disentangled them enough to walk and said, "Ride with me. Your car will be safe here." Way past any rational thought, she allowed him to lead her over to his Mercedes and put her in the passenger seat; within minutes they were pulling into her apartment complex. He hurried around the car and helped her out. Her fingers were shaking too much to find the door key, so she handed the whole set to him. He gave a shout of victory as he finally located the key and soon they were inside.

When the door closed, he reached for her and brought his lips crashing down on hers again. Gone was the questioning kiss of before; now there was only need and desire so hot that she was afraid she would burst into flames. His hands were roaming her body, desperately seeking to discover every curve. She couldn't stop the moan that escaped her lips as he cupped the heavy weight of her breasts through the thin material of her dress. Moisture was pooling between her thighs as she frantically ran her hands down his back and pulled his shirt from the waistband of his trousers.

His skin was hot to the touch, and her nails raked down his back with need. His tongue was devouring her mouth, mating with hers, and his hands were gripping her bottom, grinding against her with only a few thin layers separating them.

"Bed . . ." Jason picked her up and she clamped her legs around his hips as she pointed him to her bedroom door. Not bothering to turn on the lights, he slowly felt his way over to the bed and lowered her gently.

As he leaned over her, he asked, "Are you okay with your toe?"

She pulled him down on top of her. *Screw the toe!* He rolled over and positioned her on top of him, reaching down for the hem of her dress and slowly raising it over her head. *Thank God I wore my good underwear tonight.*

He then reached over and found the switch on the bedside lamp, and she was bathed in the dim glow. "Oh, God, you're so perfect," he purred. She had worn a pale blue lace push-up bra that made the best of her assets and a matching pair of tiny lace panties. She reached for the hem of his shirt, desperate for skin-to-skin contact but he caught her hands and stopped her. "No, not yet. I'll lose control fast when I feel you against me."

He lowered her back to the bed and knelt between her legs. He ran his hands lightly up past her thighs to her stomach. She arched up off the bed when she felt the warmth of his lips blazing the same path his hands had just touched. Slowly, his tongue swirled around her belly button and teased and slid a few inches lower. Breathless with anticipation, she almost cried out when he stopped his descent and, instead, started to work his way back up until he reached the underside of her breasts.

Jason located the front closure on her bra and deftly snapped it open. Her breasts were laid bare to his gaze. His hands cupped the weight of her as one thumb came up to stroke her nipple. "Oh, baby, you're beautiful."

Hearing a moan, she was surprised to discover it had come from her throat. Her nipples were hard and standing at attention. He lowered his head and took a nipple in his mouth, swirling his tongue over the peak.

She felt him reach down between her thighs and lightly cup her mound through the thin lace of her panties. She dug her hands into his hair, holding his mouth in place. She raised her hips to meet his questing fingers as they slid under the lace of her panties and slowly lowered them down her legs. He then glided his hand back up her legs and between her slick folds to tease her. She almost jumped from the bed, so sensitive was that throbbing part of her against the pressure of his fingers.

The sucking of his mouth on her breasts seemed to mimic the motion of his hand between her thighs. She pushed her thighs tighter against his hand, instinctively seeking release from the pressure inside her. Liquid pooled there as he slipped a finger inside her, stroking her where she needed it most.

Time ceased to have any meaning. The only focus was what was happening to her body, the unbearable pressure between her legs. She felt another finger being inserted, stroking faster as his thumb continued to rub her clit. Suddenly, feeling like she was going to break apart if he didn't stop, she started to pull back from his hand, so strong were the feelings burning in her body.

She heard Jason's voice whisper, "No, baby, let it happen. Come for me." The motion of his hand increased as did the suction at her breasts, and suddenly she was falling through space and spinning so fast there was nothing left in the world but the feeling of the contractions that shook her body. "Oh, God, baby, that's it," he said hoarsely.

Lying limply, sparks of electricity still running through her body, she felt his lips take up their earlier path, kissing her stomach and moving slowly down her body. She jerked from the shock of his lips kissing her inner thighs. As she tried to move her legs together to escape from the ultimate intimacy, she felt Jason's hand on her hip, soothing her. "Let me taste you. I need to know all of your beautiful body."

She slowly eased her legs apart to the gentle pressure of his hand. She held her breath as she felt the first light stroke of his tongue across her folds. Jason went slowly so as not to startle her and soon all thoughts of protest were gone, and there was nothing other than the exquisite feel of his tongue licking and sucking and turning her whole body into an inferno of need. She screamed as an orgasm ripped through her body and almost blacked out from the force of it.

Dimly, she was aware of Jason's clothing hitting the floor. She raised her arms to bring him back to her and felt the weight of him return, this time with no barriers between them. His skin seemed to be on fire as his mouth devoured hers. As his tongue slid past her teeth into her mouth, she felt the nudge of his erection between her thighs, seeking entrance into her body. She wrapped her legs around his waist, as his tongue thrust deeply into her mouth. At the same moment, his body pulsed into hers.

The weight and size of him took her breath away as her body tried to stretch to accommodate him. He slid slowly inch by inch until he was buried to the hilt in her. He whispered in her ear, "Are you okay?" In answer, she wrapped her legs tighter and moved her hips against his. With a groan, she felt him slide out of her and then slowly back in as if afraid he would hurt her.

She was surprised to feel the fire raging again. She wanted him to lose control, needed to feel him moving inside her, hard and fast. She gripped the firm cheeks of his tight butt and pushed him against her, forcing him deeply inside her again and finally felt the control he had been exercising snap.

Never had she felt anything like this before. She didn't know where she stopped and Jason began; together they were one. The pressure was building inside her again, small quakes shaking her as she met Jason thrust for thrust. Suddenly, he leaned back on his knees, taking her with him. He slid so deep he almost seemed to touch her cervix. He took a nipple in his mouth as his big body pounded into hers.

She was helpless to do anything other than whimper, so great was her need for release. His mouth fastened on the other nipple, sucking it inside his burning hot mouth. As she started to feel the ripples beginning inside her, she gripped Jason's shoulders, lifting herself up to meet his thrusts. He pumped harder as he felt her beginning to shudder. His mouth took hers again, his tongue swallowing the cries that erupted from her lips as spasm after spasm ripped through her body, her orgasm all-consuming. Jason stiffened against her, his head jerking back, and a hoarse cry erupted from his lips.

She felt boneless and could do nothing but limply lay against him, completely spent. He gently lifted her and laid her down on the bed. Stroking the hair off her face, he kissed her lips, no pressure now, just sweetness. Dimly, she was aware of Jason rising from the bed and discarding a condom. God, she'd been so far gone, she hadn't given protection a thought, so she was glad he'd had the presence of mind to protect them both.

After turning the lamp off, Claire felt Jason slide back in the bed and she cuddled into his arms. He brushed a kiss against her neck as she drifted off to sleep. Sometime during the night she was awoken by Jason pulling her back against him and lifting her leg over his as he slid inside her. He made slow, leisurely love to her, and again her body shattered into a million pieces with his cries of release mingling with her own.

Chapter Sixteen

Claire awoke from a peaceful sleep by the morning sunlight streaming in her window. She winced as her body ached in unusual places. Memories of the previous night came flooding in and she looked around her bedroom and wondered if it had all been a dream. She noticed the closed bathroom door and the spray from the shower was a distant sound in the background.

She couldn't believe what had happened. She'd actually slept with her boss, the hot guy she'd ogled from afar for years but never seriously considered a romantic prospect. As the sound of the water stopped, she felt herself tense up. The morning after was unfamiliar ground for her. *Buck up, girl. Here comes the walk of shame.* She grabbed a nightshirt from her drawer and slid it over her head before returning to bed.

After a few moments, the door opened and Jason walked out in his boxer briefs looking good enough to eat. She felt her mouth go dry at that thought. With her eyes averted in embarrassment, she felt the bed dip as he sat down beside her. His hand lifted her chin and warm lips descended on hers for a long, mind-numbing kiss. He gave her a lazy smile and said, "Good morning. You looked so beautiful lying there, I almost didn't have the strength to get up."

She blushed and replied shyly, "Um, good morning."

He slid his hand in her hair, massaging her scalp, and said, "I've got a meeting downtown at ten. I need to go home and grab a quick change of clothes before I go. I'm leaving tonight for Charleston for the rest of the week. Why don't you come with me? Personnel can direct my calls. Anything else that needs to be dealt with can be sent to another office for the rest of the week."

"I thought Grayson was coming here this weekend."

"That's somewhat up in the air right now. I was planning to go there for a few days, and then he was planning to come here for a few. Hopefully his schedule will still allow him to do that. He's trying to finalize a big deal so that takes precedence."

"I would love to go to Charleston, but I would need to check on my mother and there isn't time for that today," she said sadly.

He leaned down to give her another quick kiss and said, "Take today and use the time to make sure she has everything she needs. I'll pick you up about seven tonight, okay?"

"Oh . . . okay, I guess I could do that."

"Good girl. Don't worry about the office; I'll have that covered today."

Jason turned to pick up his shirt and she caught sight of his back and gasped. "Oh no!" Long red marks where fingernails had raked his back were clearly visible.

He looked at her inquiringly. "What's wrong?"

Horrified, she said, "Your back—please tell me I didn't do that to you."

With a laugh he said, "Well, the only other option is someone else did it. So, which would you prefer?"

"I'll take the credit. . . . Does it hurt?"

"It did sting a bit in the shower, but it's nothing a kiss wouldn't help," Jason said with a wicked grin.

She laughed at his hopeful expression and slid down to the end of the bed. Tentatively, she stood on her tiptoes and hooked her arms around his neck. He lowered his head but left the next step to her. She ran the tip of her tongue across the seam of his lips, seeking entrance. He obligingly opened his mouth, and she slid her tongue inside, hungry for the taste of him. With a groan he took charge of the kiss and deepened it. Soon, they were both wrapped tightly around each other and the feel of his erection pressed against her thigh. His big hand cupped her breast, rubbing the nipple to a hard pebble.

They were both reaching the point of no return when a shrill beep sounded. She looked around in confusion, wanting to destroy whatever had broken their embrace. With jerky motions, he pressed one more kiss against her swollen mouth and walked over to her dresser to pick up his phone. "It's my alarm. I set it before bed last night so I wouldn't miss the meeting this morning. I didn't trust myself to give a damn otherwise." As he clicked the alarm to silence, he grabbed his abandoned shirt and pants, making quick work of dressing.

Jason sat on the edge of the bed beside her to put his shoes on. "Can I never walk away from you without a tent in the front?" She tried to contain her amusement as she looked down at the front of his pants. "Think it's funny, huh? You aren't exactly getting off lightly either." At his pointed gaze, she saw the clear outline of her hard nipples against the front of the nightshirt. Crossing her arms over her chest, she stuck her tongue out at him. With a chuckle, he tapped her playfully on the nose and said, "I'll call you later. Be careful on your errands today." Another quick kiss and he was gone.

She lay back in bed, going over the previous night in her mind. Jason was an exceptional lover. He only took his pleasure when he was sure that she'd had hers first. His self-control seemed limitless. She'd expected the sex to be hot but was surprised at the tenderness that had been so much a part of it. In her limited experience, sex had never been that enjoyable.

Even when Suzy was raving about it, she'd wondered what all the fuss was about. Now Claire knew that she'd never been with anyone who actually cared about her pleasure. Jason had dedicated himself to her and her pleasure. Just thinking about it made her core ache with need. *Maybe it's time for a cold shower and a towel to wipe the drool.* She still had the desire to pinch herself to make sure she was awake.

Claire called Louise and explained she was going out of town on business again. Even if Louise wondered why she was suddenly traveling a lot, she didn't ask. Claire wrote down a list of supplies Louise and her mother needed and promised she would be over after lunch. She was driving downtown when a store caught her eye. She pulled into a parking space in front of a thrift store that Suzy often frequented. Excited about the week with Jason, she decided to do something she hadn't done for pleasure in years: go in a store to shop for herself.

She knew there was something ironic about buying clothes a couple of days after taking out a loan to fix her mother's roof, but for once she wanted to think of herself. For the first time in so long, she wanted to feel young and carefree for just this week. Reality would come crashing down soon enough. She entered the store and was excited to see all the beautiful clothing filling rack after rack. A pretty girl around her own age came up to her as she was looking through some dresses. "Hey there, I'm Ashley. What're we looking for today?"

Claire smiled at her and said, "I'm going to Charleston for the week, and I would like some casual clothes, something different."

With a wiggle of her eyebrows, Ashley asked, "For business or pleasure?" Taking note of Claire's blush at the question, Ashley smiled and said, "Okay, pleasure."

Soon her arms were loaded with colorful sundresses, Capri pants, and sleeveless tops. She modeled each selection for Ashley. Finally she decided on a short yellow sundress with multicolored flowers on the bottom of it and another sundress in turquoise. Her favorite was a halter dress in a beautiful emerald green that made her eyes sparkle and put her breasts proudly on display.

Ashley matched the sundresses up with cute strappy sandals and the halter dress with high-heeled wedge sandals that laced up her ankles. She also selected some shorts that showed entirely too much leg and a few pairs of Capri linen pants with matching silk tanks. Ashley even matched up costume jewelry that complemented each outfit.

Claire cringed as she waited for Ashley to ring up her purchases. She was relieved and surprised that the total was far less than she could have hoped for or expected. She thanked Ashley profusely and assured her she would be back. With a spring in her step, she left the shop humming.

So this is what being in love feels like. Wow! Where had that thought come from? It was more like being in lust. Sex with someone hardly qualified as love. Still, it was such a great feeling to have someone to want to look attractive for. She hadn't felt that way since college. The few people she'd dated since then never filled her with the desire to buy different clothing or look more feminine.

Until Jason, she'd never noticed anything lacking from her wardrobe or her social life. There was a nagging voice in the back of her mind telling her that this couldn't last, but for once, she was going to live in the moment. No matter what happened between them, she knew she would be better for having this time with Jason, even if it was only brief.

She checked her phone to see if she'd missed any calls while inside the store and saw that she had a new message. Eagerly playing it, hoping it was Jason, she was disappointed to hear Pam's voice. She wanted her to know that she had hired a new girl for the bachelor parties. When Claire had weekends available again, Pam would try to schedule some work for her. She made it clear though that her days of having all the weekend parties were over.

Maybe it was for the best. She could probably pick up a weekend clerical job at one of the area hospitals, the difference being it would require more hours than Partiez Plus had. Next week she would sign up with an employment agency and see what they had to offer.

Chapter Seventeen

Claire picked up the items on Louise's list and arrived in time for lunch. Louise had decided to make a late brunch, and she tucked into a plate of eggs and bacon with gusto. Her mother was having a good day today and the three of them remained at the table long after the meal was finished chatting and laughing. Louise asked several questions about her trip, and Claire hated not being completely truthful with her. Claire could tell by the sparkle in Louise's eyes that she suspected there was more than she was telling, but Louise didn't press her.

As she was leaving, Louise told her that her nephew would be by tomorrow to start the roof repairs. She left a check to pay him in case he finished the work before she returned home. She gave her mother and Louise one last hug and promised to call and check on them while she was away.

*   *   *

Jason was in trouble. He felt it in his gut and his gut was never wrong. The plan of getting Claire out of his system didn't seem to be working. After a night of the best sex of his life, he still wasn't remotely satisfied. In fact, he ached to be with her and inside her again. The scary part was, it wasn't just the sex he missed. He missed her. He had lain awake this morning enjoying the feel of her curled into his side, her bandaged toe resting on top of his leg, her small hands lying so trustingly on his chest. His body was screaming at him to wake her while his mind was telling him to run like hell. He practically bolted out of the bed and into the bathroom.

While in the shower, he convinced himself that the tender feelings were just because he had known and worked closely with Claire for several years, so it was only natural to feel more for her than just some one-night stand. There was no reason this couldn't work to his advantage. As his assistant, she could travel with him while they were involved and with the merger in progress no one would question the sudden need for that.

The novelty of crossing a line and sleeping with someone at the office had to be what made the sex so good, so forbidden. When the novelty wore off—as it would—they'd move on. He felt better after working everything out in his mind and decided to give Claire a call to make sure everything was still a go for Charleston. He hoped he could continue to block the voice in his head urging him to run.

When Claire arrived home from her mother's, her cell phone rang.

"Hey, beautiful, how's your day going?" Jason asked.

Her pulse kicked into high gear at the sound of his voice, but she tried to sound cool. "Hey, it's going great. How about yours?"

"No problems, everything is on schedule." She wondered if anything ever dared to go off schedule where Jason was concerned.

"Did you get someone lined up to cover the office while we're away?"

"Yes, everything is taken care of. How is your mother doing today?"

"She's good, actually. I had lunch with her and Louise earlier, and she was her old self."

"That's great. I'm glad you had that time. I'm going to work from my home the rest of the afternoon. I've got several conference calls lined up and I need to pack as well. I should be free a bit earlier, so how about I pick you up around six?"

"Okay, I'll see you then."

"Oh and, Claire, I've missed you today." Not waiting for a reply, Jason clicked off after that comment.

She felt warmth flood through her. She had, of course, missed him terribly today but was shocked to hear him admit that he felt the same way. She couldn't delude herself into thinking that this was anything more than sex to Jason. This wasn't a fairy tale and he wouldn't be taking her off to his castle. He was, however, taking her off to Charleston, where she would have the rest of the week to pretend—just for a little while—that her Prince Charming had finally arrived.

She was surprised to hear her phone ringing again. She quickly answered it thinking that Jason had forgotten something. As soon as she said hello, she cringed as Suzy said, "Well, well, well, is someone finally getting laid?" Despite being horrified at the question, she couldn't contain her laughter and it burst out. No matter how crude or shocking Suzy could be at times, you still had to laugh at some of the things that came out of her mouth.

"What're you talking about?" she hedged.

With a dramatic sigh, Suzy said, "Really, from all the choices out there, you're choosing the dumb route? That's just disappointing. Honey, you know I'm wired into everything at Danvers, right down to when everyone takes a leak every day. Do you really think I haven't heard that Jason requested a fill in for the office because he needed his assistant to travel with him this week? Now, I may have been able to buy into it if I hadn't run into him in the elevator this morning. That man had the 'Oh so satisfied, I've been done left and right' look all over his face. Men can't fake that shit. He was fresh out of the sack with someone. So . . . he was either fresh out of your sack and you're going with him this week for more nookie, or he was fresh off someone else's sheets and you're actually going to work," Suzy finished smugly.

"Oh, Suz, you missed your calling somewhere in life. You should have been a detective or a comedian. I'm not sure which," she said and laughed.

"Looks like you're admitting to option one, am I right? You know I'm going to need some details. I've been wondering what was under the hood of that baby for a while." Claire had never been in the position to kiss and tell before, and it was a strange feeling. She knew she could trust anything she said to Suzy not to go further, but it was still hard to talk about something so private and special.

"Er . . . yes, there's been some new developments there," she admitted.

"New developments—like are we talking about the weather or some hot, sweaty sex?"

She finally gave in with a sigh, knowing she would never get off the phone otherwise. "Okay, we slept together and, oh my God, Suz, it was wonderful. He was just . . . wonderful."

With a snort, Suzy said, "Yada, yada! Let's get over the G-rated version and answer such hard-hitting questions as, was it good? Was it big? Did he go for quality or quantity?"

As her face started to flame, she lay back against the couch cushions and answered, "It was great. It was big and quality all the way, both times."

"Yessss," Suzy squealed, "I knew it! So you're going with him this week for more, huh?"

"Yes, he asked me to go. He's picking me up at six tonight."

"Well, honey, if anyone ever needed a good bang, it's you." Suzy laughed.

"You're terrible, Suz, really you are."

"Claire," Suzy began, a serious tone entering her voice, "I'm all for getting out there and test driving some new models. I can't imagine a finer model than Jason, but be careful, okay?"

"What're you saying, Suz?"

"I'm just saying that people like Jason are different. I'm sure he has a lot of experience with women, but I don't think he's looking to settle down anytime soon."

"I know, but thank you for caring enough to point it out."

"Sure thing. Now get out there and have some fun for both of us."

"I will. You know you could still come for the weekend and see Grayson if you change your mind."

"I'm not looking for a pretty boy. How do all these hunks like Jason and Pretty Boy have all that money at their age? Oh well, guess it's better to be a rich young stud than an old dude, right? Have fun and call me when you get home. I need more details—lots more of them."

With a laugh, she agreed and finally got off the phone without having to give out Jason's underwear size. The clock showed three by then, plenty of time for a nap. Soon she was dropping off to sleep, dreaming of Jason's hands sliding over her body, and even in sleep her heart melted just a little more.

Chapter Eighteen

Jason knocked at the door just as Claire was bringing her garment bag and overnight case into the living room. She was wearing the yellow sundress she'd purchased earlier. She thought it would be both comfortable and dressy enough to get by if they decided to stop along the way. Due to her injured toe, she was also donning flip-flops again. Luckily it seemed to be much better, and it looked as if it would heal without losing the nail. He had also opted to travel in comfort and was sporting low-riding, well-worn jeans and a white polo. *Yummy.*

He brushed a kiss against her lips as he came into her apartment, and it quickly turned into a full-fledged love affair of the mouth. When they pulled apart several minutes later, both were breathing hard, and he whispered against her ear, "How was your day?"

Barely able to think rationally after the kiss, she replied, "Um . . . it was good. I had a nap and then ran late packing and couldn't find my other shoe." Jason was smiling as her nervous rambling ended. He reached over to pick up her cases and then opened the door. She locked up and followed him to his car.

Billy was walking to his car as Jason was storing her luggage. She was surprised to see him walk over to Jason and extend his hand. "Hey, man, good to see you again. You guys going somewhere?"

"Yes, Claire is going to be away for a few days. I would really appreciate it if you'd keep an eye on her place."

"Oh sure, man. Billy will make sure no one bothers anything—don't worry."

"Thanks," Jason replied.

Billy turned and said a quick hello to her and was on his way. "That was weird. I've never known Billy to miss an opportunity to talk. He seemed almost normal."

"Yes, well, maybe he has finally figured out that people don't like being accosted on their way in and out of their home."

"Maybe," she said doubtfully. She asked Jason where they'd be staying in Charleston.

Jason replied, "I thought you'd enjoy the historic district. Have you been there?"

"No, I haven't, but I've always wanted to."

"There's a great hotel that I've stayed in before. Their service is excellent and the privacy is unsurpassed."

She had to wonder how many other women had

benefited from the privacy offered at this hotel. As if sensing her thoughts, he added, "I've only stayed there when in town on business, so it will be nice to enjoy it on a personal level, as well."

With a bright smile of relief, she said, "It sounds perfect. I can't wait. Will you be working at Mericom each day?"

"I'll go in for meetings but won't spend a full day there. I would love for you to come along as well to give me your opinion of their operation."

"I'd like that," she said shyly.

"Grayson will be spending quite a lot of time at Danvers as the merger nears and even afterwards. Charleston will remain his base for a while, but he'll have an expanded role within Danvers. I look forward to having a strong person to shoulder some of the day-to-day load that the merger will create."

She was surprised that he would admit to needing assistance, much less be willing to relinquish some of his control at Danvers to Grayson. "Grayson also has a brother, Nicholas, who you will meet while we're there. He primarily does the traveling for Mericom, so he isn't in the office as much as Grayson. He'll also assume a big role in daily operations when the merger is complete and will travel considerably less."

"I'd no idea Mericom was going to change Danvers this much. I guess I assumed it would be the other way around."

"Danvers will be too big to manage without some

changes. They'll all be for the better though: We will hire more staff for our office, and some will also transfer between the two companies when the merger is complete.

"We will dine tomorrow night at Grayson's home. I want you to be comfortable with him and, of course, Nicholas, since you will communicate with them both a great deal in the future." She would like to think he meant that as his companion she would see them more. Somehow, she knew he meant it strictly in the professional sense. *Did you think he was going to ask you to go steady a day after sleeping with him, silly?*

She was startled but pleased when she felt Jason lay his hand over her hand and link his fingers with hers. "I'm glad you came. I would have never been able to concentrate with you so far away," he admitted. She had no words for the way his statement made her feel, so she squeezed his hand instead, letting him know that she felt the same way. He said, "I thought we could have a late dinner when we arrive. How does seafood sound to you?"

"Mmm, that sounds great. I love seafood, and I bet it's wonderful there." The rest of the drive passed quickly, with conversation flowing as if they'd been together for years, which, in fact, in some capacity, they had been.

The restaurant that Jason had selected was in the battery district of Charleston, on the waterfront. As they pulled up a valet carefully opened her door and assisted her out. Jason handed the keys to another valet as they walked toward the entrance of the restaurant. He had obviously planned ahead and made a reservation since they were quickly escorted to a table overlooking the water. "This is lovely, Jason. I'd no idea Charleston was so beautiful."

"This is only a small part of the appeal of Charleston. I look forward to showing you the city before we leave. Perhaps tonight, if you feel up to it, we will take a stroll on the waterfront before we go to the hotel."

"Oh yes, please, I would love that." She asked Jason for suggestions on the menu and was relieved when he offered to order a local favorite for them.

When the waiter returned, he selected the she-crab soup for an appetizer and the lobster Newburg with fresh vegetables and wild rice as the main course. It sounded mouthwatering and she was embarrassed to hear her stomach growl in appreciation. Jason apparently heard it as well. He looked at the waiter and said, "Could you please bring a basket of bread with our soup? My lady is hungry."

She playfully stuck her tongue out at him as the waiter left the table. "Don't give me ideas, Claire. I find I can think of many things I would like to do with that tongue of yours." The desire in his gaze was unmistakable.

She leaned forward and bravely said, "I hope you will show me some of them later."

"If you look at me like that much longer, I'll show you right now on this table, and I don't really fancy getting arrested tonight, so we'd better behave ourselves for now."

They chatted quietly about the upcoming merger and also about their plans for the week. When the main course arrived she was delighted to see the delicate puffed pastry filled with a cream sauce and slices of lobster. "This looks fabulous. I've never tried this before."

"It's one of my favorites, especially when it's a specialty of the house, as it is here."

After the main course, she finally pushed her plate back, surprised to find it was almost empty. The combination of food, the wine, and the company was hard to resist. She felt Jason's hand on her leg as he asked if she would like dessert and coffee. "No, I couldn't possibly eat another bite. I would like to walk for a bit though, if it's okay with you." In minutes he had paid the check and they were walking hand in hand on the waterfront. "This is like one of those perfect moments in time that you read about."

"Yes, indeed it is," Jason replied as he stopped and pulled her into his embrace. His thumb stroked over the bottom of her lip, and she reached her tongue out and teasingly touched it.

Jason's breath seemed to catch in his chest, and he crushed her in his embrace. Gone was the gentleness of a few moments ago. Now it was as if a fire raged inside of him that had gotten out of control. His lips took possession of hers, his tongue staking a claim to every recess of her mouth, touching, seeking, devouring. He jerked his head back, taking several deep breaths as he pulled his hand through his hair.

"If we don't stop now, I'm going to have you against that seawall in about thirty seconds. Let's walk back and get the car. I think it's past time to find our room." She almost laughed as Jason rushed them both to the car at top speed.

The drive to the hotel was done in similar fashion. They were checked in quickly and were soon in the room. Jason had his arms around her, and they pressed against the wall before the door clicked shut.

"You don't know how bad I've wanted to do this. I didn't think dinner would ever end," he groaned.

He picked her up and was walking toward the bed when a knock sounded at the door. He halted in his tracks. "Damn, this had better be good." Reluctantly setting her back on her feet, he took a moment to straighten his clothing and yanked the door open.

The valet took a quick look at Jason's hard stare and quickly handed him a message. "I'm sorry, sir. This message should have been given to you when you checked in." With a curt nod of thanks, Jason shut the door and opened the note.

He grabbed his cell phone, quickly checking something and looked at her. "I'm sorry—there's a problem at a customer site with one of our components and they're threatening to cancel their entire order."

"Is it Lynwood?" she asked. Lynwood was a new customer Danvers had recently acquired and their first purchase was in the millions of dollars.

"Yeah, that's the one. I don't know how this has been screwed up, but they're livid. I need to see what the problem is and try to smooth it over."

"What can I do to help?"

Jason, already walking over to the hotel room desk, punched in numbers on his phone.

"Let me see what's going on, and we will go from there."

Chapter Nineteen

Claire walked over to a chair and sat down. She was far enough away to give Jason some privacy but close enough to offer assistance, if needed. After several phone calls, he seemed to reach the person in charge at Lynwood. He put his hand over the phone and asked, "Claire, could you possibly look in my briefcase—over next to our luggage—and see if you can locate the files on Lynwood?" She walked toward the bedroom and located Jason's briefcase and started looking through a stack of folders for anything on Lynwood.

She pulled out two folders and continued to thumb through the remainder when a name caught her eye. Confused, she wondered why he would have a file on her in his briefcase. With her curiosity getting the better of her, she opened the folder and stared at the contents in shock, unable to grasp what she was seeing. She thumbed through copies of her loan application from Danvers, as well as a copy of the check issued to her.

A note was attached to the check copy from the credit union.

Mr. Danvers, per your instructions, I wanted to advise you that Claire Walters did apply for a loan of $5,000 today. As per your directive, the loan was approved immediately and the funds made available the next day. Ms. Walters did inquire about repayment of the loan, and I convinced her that her payments were deferred for 6 months, due to a special promotion. These funds were issued from your personal account as requested.

On the next page, Claire found an e-mail from Pam at Partiez Plus. Almost unable to process any further information, she made herself read the e-mail.

Dear Mr. Danvers,

It was a pleasure and somewhat of a surprise to hear from you concerning an employee. I was never informed that Claire was under contract to Danvers and that the contract precluded outside employment of our specific specialty. Claire is a valued member of our staff, and as such it is with great regret that I'll need to replace her. I do, however, understand and commend your need to protect the employment and benefits of a key employee. I will as you requested keep this matter confidential and will notify Claire of my intentions to

fill her position. I cannot thank you enough for recom-
mending Partiez Plus to Mr. and Mrs. Smythe. Their
business will be invaluable.

   Please let me know if I can be of any further assis-
tance.

Claire felt numb, her mind desperately looking for
another explanation for what she'd read. He was behind the scenes of her life and directing it like a play.
Her turn of good fortune was not actually fortune at all.
It was Jason pulling the strings, taking over, and making her into someone he deemed acceptable. The sense
of betrayal—on so many levels—was overwhelming.
At the center was Jason. Leslie the creditor of course
owed her loyalty to Jason and, even though ethically it
was wrong, she probably felt as if she were doing Claire
a favor.

   Pam, in her estimation, was as guilty as Jason. She'd
basically sold out to him for his contacts. After years of
working for her and developing what she thought was
a friendship between them, Pam had betrayed her confidence and privacy by discussing her employment
with Jason. It was obvious from her e-mail that she'd
no intention of using her any longer despite her assurances to Claire that she would have the opportunity to
work future parties.

   What other problems had Jason decided to solve for
her? Were her mother and Louise now on their way to
live in Florida with his aunt Ella? Would she come

home to a new house herself? Surely, someone living in an apartment wasn't good enough for the mighty Jason Danvers to sleep with. Well, that was no longer something he would have to worry about. She was finished with him and finished with Danvers. Word had probably already spread there by now that she was Jason's kept woman.

"Claire, what's keeping you? Did you find the file?" Jason asked from the next room. Rage burned through her, causing her hands to shake as she gripped the file. She stalked back into the sitting area and smacked the folder with her name on it down in front of him.

He gave her a questioning look at the abrupt gesture. He balanced the telephone on his shoulder as he opened the file, not noticing the name on the front. She recognized the exact moment when he became aware of what he was looking at. His speech stopped midsentence, and he closed his eyes briefly as if in resignation. "I'll have to call you back," he said into the cell phone. He disconnected the call and turned to face her.

She waited for him to defend himself, to say anything, but he continued to sit and study her, seeming to be waiting for her to say something. "Well, surely you have something to say? You've had plenty to say to everyone else concerning me, so why not to me in person?"

"Claire, you're upset. Let's leave this until you're feeling rational enough to listen to reason."

The tone of his voice, as if he were humoring a child,

infuriated her further. "I want you to explain what the hell you thought you were doing invading my privacy and taking over my life."

"If we must do this now while I'm in the middle of a major problem, at least sit down so that we may discuss this like adults."

"Fine," she snapped, and perched on the edge of a wingback chair across the room. "Well? I'm waiting."

After taking a deep breath, he stared at her and asked quietly, "What is it that you want me to say, Claire?" If possible, the question stroked her rage to an even higher level. It was as if this whole conversation was a nuisance to him, and he couldn't see what she could possibly be upset over.

"Okay . . . let's go in order. How about explaining the loan from Danvers, which apparently wasn't a loan at all? Then we can work our way to my job with Partiez Plus that you got me fired from. Am I missing anything, or is there something else not in the folder? Do I have a new home now that I'm not aware of or maybe my mother has free medication for life?" Breathing quickly, she saw an answering anger start to burn in Jason's blue eyes.

"Listen, I don't really have time for this right now and I never took you for such a drama queen. I fail to see what could possibly have you so enraged. I gave you help when you needed it and were too proud to ask. I would have done the same for any employee. Since when is it a crime to help someone?"

"You didn't offer help. You made choices for me. I don't need handouts, and I'm perfectly capable of handling my own affairs. I told you that when you brought this up in your office, yet you ignored everything I said and decided you knew best. Poor stupid Claire couldn't possibly be able to think for herself, right?"

He jumped to his feet and stalked over to her chair, glaring down at her. "Oh yes, I can see how great you were doing at handling your own problems. Being a stripper for a room full of horny men is always the answer to every girl's problems. I thought you were being forced to do that because of money, but maybe I was wrong. Maybe it was for pleasure all along. Do you get some type of thrill from parading around half-naked and turning on a bunch of strangers? Maybe you just like to play the blushing virgin during the day."

She flew out of the chair and her hand landed hard against his cheek, the red imprint clearly visible. "Go to hell! What I do or why I do it is none of your concern!" she yelled.

Harsh laughter erupted from Jason's chest as he reached out and hauled her against his chest. "That's where you're wrong. Everything you do is of interest to me. If that makes me a bastard, then so be it."

His lips swooped down on hers, crushing the protests bubbling from her lips. She tried to turn her head to escape his plundering lips, but his hands reached up and locked her in place. His tongue moved insistently along the seam of her lips, not asking, but demanding entrance into her mouth. With a groan, she felt her body betraying her. Her lips seemed to part of their own accord. He took possession, his tongue stabbing inside to claim the victory.

He moved his hands from her face and slid them down to her hips. He gripped her bottom, pulling her roughly against him, leaving little doubt as to how excited he was. Her own hands locked around his neck, bringing her body into even closer contact with his hard contours, desperate to feel his heat everywhere. Jason's hand slid back up her body and continued on until it was cupping her breast.

She arched her back as he lowered his head to suck her nipple through the fabric of her dress and bra. Heat exploded inside her. The cool feel of the wet fabric against her nipple was almost more erotic than being nude. Dimly in the background the voice in her head was screaming in protest. But her body was burning in need and the voice was easily overlooked. She couldn't remember why she was angry with him; she could only focus on the need building inside her.

Her hands lowered to the buckle of Jason's belt, and she soon had it open. The snap of his jeans was next. He slid his hands up her thighs, bunching the material of the short dress around her waist. He gripped the flimsy material of her panties, and she felt them give on the side sliding down her legs. Quickly kicking them off her feet, she moaned as his hands slid between her legs and into the drenching heat within.

She was wet and ready, her need for him so obvious that it should have been embarrassing. The approving groan from Jason made her forget that thought. She basked instead in the answering excitement she felt rippling through him as his body shuddered with arousal. As if unable to hold back any longer, he quickly stepped out of his jeans and leaned back against the wall. He lifted her up and then lowered her onto him, filling her completely.

She wrapped her legs around his waist. Her head fell back, and he kissed his way up to her neck as he pumped into her. Her body almost immediately crested an orgasm. She screamed and convulsed around him, her orgasm seeming to be never-ending as he continued to slide in and out of her. Jason grabbed her tightly as he walked over to a chair, careful to keep them connected. He sat down, arranging her legs on either side of his as he continued to pump into her. He took one nipple into his mouth, sucking, while his other hand roamed her body.

She thought she might faint, so great was the pleasure rushing through her. The room was filled with the sounds of their labored breathing and moans of pleasure. He used this new position to his advantage, and his hands seemed to be everywhere at once. He stroked her clit and what little strength she felt left her completely. Jason took her hips and moved her up and down on his length, driving them both toward completion.

She didn't think it was even possible to have an orgasm stronger than the last, but she found that she was very wrong. The pressure in her body suddenly exploded white-hot, pushing a scream from her that was quickly echoed and swallowed by Jason's mouth. She felt him reach his own release, and she fell limply against him, all coherent thought completely gone.

Dimly, she was aware of him separating their bodies, and then she was lying on something soft as he curled around her back, his arm resting against her stomach. The last thought in her mind before she drifted away was that there was truly a thin line between love and hate.

Claire awoke sometime later, disoriented as she looked around the unfamiliar room. The clock beside the bed glowed, showing the hour of 7:00 a.m. Stretching, she felt the aches and pains in her body and smiled at the memory of how she'd gotten them. Looking beside her, she could make out the indentation on the pillow where Jason had lain. That side was now empty and cool to the touch. He had been up for some time.

Suddenly a memory intruded on her happiness, and the evening before came crashing back. *Oh God, no!* Jason was no better than her father. He had taken over her life. The packaging might be different, but the rest was the same. She could hear her father's mocking voice in her head as though it were yesterday.

Poor, stupid Claire. Do you honestly think that you, your

mother, or your sister would ever survive on your own?
You're barely fit to leave the house, everything you do is
wrong. I'm left taking care of you bunch of fools. If I can ever
even manage to get anyone to marry you, I truly pity him.
Not only are you plain; you have a complete lack of intelli-
gence. You and your sister got that from your mother, the
only idiot I know bigger than you two. Sure, you go to college
now, and when you fail—as you will—don't think you can
crawl back to me to take care of you.

She pulled Jason's pillow against her chest and
wept. She cried for herself for the first time ever. She
cried for the years of torment and abuse at the hands of
a man who should have never been a husband or a father. She cried for the loss of her sister, who never had
a chance to spread her wings, and for her mother, who
had stayed with her father as if she deserved no better.
Lastly, she cried for the broken hopes and dreams she'd
allowed herself to have about Jason.

He seemed so different. In the time she had worked
for him he had praised her work and rarely questioned
anything she'd done for him. He always treated everyone with respect, even when there was a problem. She
was blindsided by the part of him she'd discovered
yesterday. So great was her trust in him, she almost felt
like she'd imagined the whole thing.

Maybe she could even find some way to deal with
the loan he had engineered on her behalf, since she'd
applied for it of her own free will. Contacting Pam and
dangling a wealthy new client over her if she termi-

nated Claire was something that she could find no way around. This reeked of something her father would have done. Had her second occupation so embarrassed Jason that he couldn't imagine himself sleeping with someone who jumped out of a cake? Yet she had never found him to be arrogant or snobbish; quite the opposite actually.

Chapter Twenty

She jerked as she felt a hand on her back. As she pulled herself up, she kept the pillow in front of her for coverage and attempted to wipe the tears from her face. Jason looked at her with concern in his blue eyes.

"Claire, baby, I've got some news for you, and I need you to stay calm," he began. She wasn't sure what she'd been expecting him to say, but this was not it. Her eyes flew to his face, alarm starting to take over.

"What? What's wrong?"

He took both her hands in his, as if to brace her. "Baby, it's your mother. She's been taken to the hospital."

"Wha . . . What? No, that can't be right. She's at home with Louise."

"I just talked to Suzy because Louise called her. When Louise couldn't reach you on your cell phone, she used Suzy's number that you'd programmed for her for emergencies and she called her." As her hands started to shake, he gripped them tighter and said,

"The car is being brought around now. If you can throw some clothes on, we will be out of here within five minutes. I'll get you to her."

Still stunned, she looked at him and asked, "What happened to her?"

"From what Suzy could gather, she passed out and Louise couldn't get her to wake up. Suzy is on her way there now and will give us an update when she knows something. Baby, let me help you get dressed. You're in shock."

She let him lead her around like a child. For one time in her life she was grateful to have someone take care of her. He pulled a top and pants from her bag, as well as undergarments, and began putting the fresh clothes on her. By the time he was finished, a valet had arrived and the room was quickly packed up. Their suitcases were taken down and packed in the car. Before she could even catch her breath, they were on the road leaving Charleston and headed for the hospital. Jason reached over and curled his fingers around hers, shooting her worried glances from time to time.

"Are you all right?" He asked in concern.

"I wish I knew what happened. She's been good lately, better than usual. I would have never left if I'd believed anything could possibly happen to her. Louise must be so scared. I have to get to them, Jason. I have to."

"We're going as fast as I dare. I promise we will be there soon." He pulled his cell phone from his pocket and passed it over to her. "Why don't you try to call

Suzy? Maybe she's found out something by now? If she's with Louise, you could speak to her as well."

With an audible breath, she dialed Suzy and prayed she would answer. "Hello?"

"Suz, it's me. Are you at the hospital yet? Do you know what's going on?" she asked urgently.

"I just had to threaten that old witch at the nurse's station, but I finally got a few answers. They're still doing tests but, sweetie, they think she might have had a stroke. They're also trying to rule out other things, but that seems to be the strong contender at this point. She's awake but very sedated. That's all I know."

"A stroke . . . How could that happen? She just had a checkup and they said everything was fine."

"Sometimes they just happen. I don't think they can predict them. Louise is here beside me now. I'm going to pass you to her. I'll hold down the fort. Be careful."

The sound of Louise's voice brought her to tears once again. "Honey, I'm so sorry. I don't know what happened to Evelyn. We were walking to the kitchen to have some breakfast, and she seemed just fine. Suddenly, she stopped, and I looked back to see what was keeping her. She had a funny look on her face and when I reached out to take her arm, she just crumpled to the floor. I didn't even have time to break her fall, it was so sudden. I tried to wake her up for a few minutes, and then I got my wits together and called nine-one-one. She never woke up, Claire. Why didn't she wake up? I rode in the ambulance with her. They said she still had a strong heartbeat, and that I should relax and let them do their job. I just want to see her to know she's okay."

Claire could hear the tears in Louise's voice much as she could feel her own. She tried to compose herself, to be strong for Louise. "It's going to be okay. I'm on my way, and I'll be there soon, and we will find out what's going on. Please stay calm. I know you did everything you could. I'm sorry I wasn't there for you."

"Oh, honey, you don't worry about that. You can't plan these things. It would have happened just as easily with you at your apartment or at work, so don't be thinking that. I love you, and I'll see you when you get here."

She softly clicked the button to end the call and handed the phone back to Jason. As she felt his hand return to hers, all the reasons she was mad at him seemed to pale. She knew that she would have to end what was between them soon. She'd think of that later. Right now she needed to feel loved even if it was all a lie.

Jason clasped Claire's hand again, trying to infuse some of his strength into her. She looked so pale and fragile. He knew from her that her mother had many health problems and, even though he would never admit it to her, he was very much afraid that this was something serious.

This crisis had delayed what he was sure would

have been another big blow-up this morning between them. He wasn't naive enough to believe that just because they had sex—mind-blowing sex, actually—that the argument was over. When she confronted him last night with that damn folder, he had suddenly been deadly afraid of losing her and whatever they had between them. It wasn't that he didn't want a serious relationship; there had just never been anyone with whom he felt the need to pursue one, until now.

Claire, to put it mildly, had knocked him on his ass. He wanted to be with her, missed her when she wasn't around, and desired her like he had never desired another woman. The need for her hadn't lessened; if anything, it had intensified each time they were together. She was a constant ache that he never seemed to be able to rid himself of. He only truly felt at peace when she was lying in his arms. He couldn't pinpoint the exact moment when he knew he loved her; it was just there.

With that love also came certain fears. Fear of losing her. Fear of not being loved in return. Fear of uncharted territory. He'd spent his life making problems go away. He solved them in business. He solved them for his parents and for Ella. He couldn't understand how he had so offended Claire. She couldn't honestly want to shoulder the burden when he could make it all go away. He wanted to take care of her, wanted her to have no worries.

He would see that her mother got the best treatment

available, and if she wanted to remain in her home, he would have it repaired and hire someone to live with her. Possibly he had overstepped the bounds a bit by talking with Pam, but surely she would see that it was all for her. The realization that he loved her made him never want to see another tear in her eyes.

Chapter Twenty-one

Claire was relieved to see they were now close to home.
Jason had broken every speed limit and they arrived at
the hospital faster than she could have dared hope.
She'd used the drive to compose herself. She needed to
be strong for her mother and for Louise.

Jason led her to the emergency section of the hospital, where they found Louise and Suzy sitting side by
side with hands clasped. Claire rushed forward, and
Suzy stood to greet her. "Hey, guys, have you heard
anything new?" she asked anxiously.

Louise rose and took her hand. "The doctor just talked
to us. He's certain now that Evelyn had a stroke. Her
speech has been affected and there's some facial drooping. He says she's stable now, but it will be several days
before they can really assess the extent of the damage."

She felt Jason's arm go around her for support and
was grateful to lean into him. "When can I see her?"

"We don't know yet. We haven't been able to get a
straight answer on that."

Jason moved Claire to a chair and lowered her into it. "Let me see what I can find out, ladies. I'll be right back."

Claire, Louise, and Suzy all sat close together with their hands clasped. Suzy looked at Louise, then at Claire and said, "Claire, I've been trying to convince Louise to let me drop her at home for some rest. She's been here for hours and I know she's tired."

"No, you don't worry about me. I'm not going anywhere until one of us gets to see Evelyn and knows she's okay." Claire knew by the stubborn set of her mouth that trying to talk to her was pointless.

"Suz, thanks for calling and coming here. I felt so much better knowing Louise wasn't alone."

"It's not a problem. Some of these doctors are complete studs. I might start hanging out here in my spare time. Can you see me as a doctor's wife? Maybe a plastic surgeon, so I can get some really big knockers, right?" Claire and Louise both laughed.

Leave it to Suzy to find a way to lighten the mood. Jason walked down the hall at that exact moment and raised a brow. "Okay, ladies, 'fess up. Am I the cause of the laughter?" Still smiling, Jason took the seat beside Claire and automatically linked his hand with hers—a move noticed by both Louise and Suzy.

"Nope, sorry. We can laugh at you later though, if you don't want to feel left out," Suzy said.

Claire turned to him. "Did you find out anything?"

"Unless there's a problem, they're going to move her out to ICU from emergency in about an hour. After she's moved, they'll allow one person at a time to go back for no more than ten minutes until visiting hours end at eight."

"Hey, cool," Suzy said. "That's a good sign that they plan to move her. Why don't we all go down and grab something to drink and maybe a bite for Ms. Louise here?" Despite Louise's protests, they all went to the cafeteria and bought coffee and sandwiches.

Even though she was trying to put on a brave front, Claire was terrified inside. Would her mother be able to recover with all the other health problems she had in addition to the stroke? As if sensing how she was feeling, Jason lifted a hand to rub along her back, soothing her tight muscles. Suzy made an effort to keep everyone entertained as Claire kept a close check on her watch, wanting to be back for a visit with her mother.

Louise took the time to quiz Jason on everything she could think of. She seemed to have given him her unofficial seal of approval by the time they were finished.

They emptied their trays and went to the ICU unit. After checking with the nurses' station, Claire was given her mother's room number and reminded again that she could visit for only ten minutes. With a squeeze of her hand for encouragement, Jason released her and escorted Suzy and Louise to the waiting room while she went down the hall to locate her mother's room.

Claire came to a stop and her hand flew to her mouth when she saw her mother. Covered with wires and tubes, Claire's mother had a tube in her mouth while her arms and hands had IVs taped in place. Wires peeked out from the top of her hospital gown. A nurse was standing beside the bed, checking her pulse rate and recording her vitals.

Claire walked slowly forward, trying to get her emotions under control. The nurse turned and gave her a warm smile. "Hi there, I'm just finishing up here. Are you Ms. Walters' daughter? My name is Glenda, and I'll be your mother's nurse, so you will see me a lot."

"Yes . . . yes, I am. I'm Claire Walters. How . . . how is she doing? Should there be this many things connected to her?"

"It's pretty normal for a stroke victim. The doctor will assess her daily, and she'll be gradually removed from some of the monitors as she improves. I know it looks really scary, but it's normal at this point," Glenda assured her.

"Has she been awake recently?"

"Not since she's been moved here. They have her sedated. It can be very confusing and upsetting for someone who has suffered a stroke to be faced with any speech or movement issues so soon afterward. The doctors want to make sure they're on hand and that they have a good idea of what they're looking at before they risk the patient possibly doing further injury in a state of panic."

"Do they believe, then, that she'll have permanent damage as a result of the stroke?"

"Oh, it's really too soon to tell. Your mother may have problems that resolve themselves over time. Whatever point she's at, it will improve to some level. It's too soon to speculate though, so I'm just going to finish my rounds and let you have your visit. Please ask for me at the nurses' station if you have any problems. Each of my patients becomes my family, and I believe in taking care of family."

Claire was really touched by the sincerity she heard in Glenda's voice, and she thanked her as the nurse closed the door on her way out.

She tentatively walked to her mother's side, her heart pounding as each step brought her closer. She gently touched her mom's hand, careful not to cause the IV to move.

Oh, Mom, you didn't deserve this. After all you have gone through in your life, was it too much to ask for some happiness? I'm sorry I wasn't here for you. I promise we will get you what you need. You will get better. God, please don't let me lose my mommy.

She felt tears rolling down her cheeks and brushed them away, almost surprised to feel them. She placed her lips gently against her mother's forehead and whispered, "I love you." She knew her ten minutes were long since over and that Louise would want to visit before visiting hours ended. When she had composed herself once again, she located the ICU waiting room and looked at the anxious faces waiting for her.

Jason walked over to slide his arm around her shoulders as she relayed the information that Glenda had given her. Suzy offered to walk Louise down to Evelyn's room.

Jason led Claire to a chair and took the one beside her. "How are you? What can I do to help you right now?"

Gripping his hand, she turned to him. "She just looked so still and there were so many things connected to her. Is she going to be okay, Jason? Is she?"

"Shhhh, it's going to be okay. We will get her everything she needs. If she's anything like you, then she's very strong and that will help her more than anything. You need to get some rest so you can be strong for her.

"When Suzy and Louise come back, we all need to go home. I want you to stay with me, Claire. I don't think you should be alone."

"No, I need to stay with Louise. She shouldn't be by herself right now."

"I meant for her to stay as well. I've got plenty of room, and my house is closer to the hospital."

When Suzy and Louise returned, Claire talked to Louise about the overnight arrangements. "Oh no, honey, my sister, Janet, is going to stay with me at the house. I hope you don't mind, but I would just feel better being there to keep an eye on the place and, well, it's my home. Suzy said she would drop me off on her way home."

"That's fine, Louise. You know I don't mind, and I understand." Claire thanked Suzy and gave her a hug.

Chapter Twenty-two

Jason guided her out the door and settled her back into his car. A short ride later, he turned into a long driveway lined with trees. Curious as to where he lived, Claire was surprised to see a beautiful two-story Craftsman-style home. He pulled into the garage and walked around the car to help her out. He pointed toward a door on the far wall and said, "I normally go in that door, which leads into the kitchen. We will use the front entrance, though, so your first view of the house isn't my messy kitchen." With a smile, she followed as he led her down a flagstone walkway that curved from the garage to the front of the house.

Lights illuminated the landscape and the stunning timber peaks that framed a huge glass door. Green plants in pots accented against the beautiful backdrop. He took her arm as he led her up the steps and inserted his key into the lock.

Jason opened the door and ushered her in before him. She blinked as light suddenly flooded the entryway and the living area beyond. She was immediately drawn to the tall, soaring ceilings with exposed beams and recessed lighting. A large modern chandelier was suspended in the middle of ceiling, giving off a soft glow. The entire front of the room was a wall of windows with a stunning view of the Atlantic Ocean taking center stage.

A fireplace surrounded by built-in cabinets flanked one wall, giving the room two distinct focal points. A comfortable-looking brown leather sofa and matching wingback chairs were placed on an area rug. Beautiful oak flooring gleamed brightly under the light. He looked strangely nervous as he waited for Claire's reaction.

"Jason, it's beautiful. I've never seen a house like this before and I love it."

A smile lit up his face as if she'd just praised his child. "I designed this house and had it built. I spent so long trying to decide exactly what I wanted in a home, somewhere I would want to live forever. I put every room together piece by piece."

With a sheepish look, he added, "This house has been home since the moment I stepped inside when it was finished. I'm so glad you like it. I used to live in the penthouse above our floor at the office, but now that's usually only for visitors, unless I'm just too tired to drive here. Let me show you the rest, and then I'll fix a quick dinner."

He led her toward an opening to the left, and she

entered a large, airy kitchen in a pale taupe color. A huge island dominated the center of the room with the kitchen cabinets and granite countertops running the length of the back wall. A breakfast nook was situated at another wall of glass with the beautiful view of the ocean clearly visible. The kitchen island displayed a loaf of bread, a plate, and some fresh fruit. She found it endearing to imagine Jason actually fixing his own meals without a housekeeper to help.

A staircase leading to the second floor was just off the kitchen, and he gave her a quick tour of two bedrooms. One of the rooms was being used as an office and the other a guest bedroom. Each had a bath attached. The oak floors and the taupe wall color continued upstairs.

They returned downstairs where he showed her a formal dining room with seating for ten and a beautiful buffet piece on the wall behind it. A round window showed a view of the front yard of the house. Going back through the living area, they went down a hallway and he opened a door to a guest bath before continuing to the master bedroom.

Even though she thought the living area was breathtaking, it paled in comparison to the bedroom. After entering through a large sitting area with pale blue walls she thought to herself, *Now, this is the rich guy's man cave.* A huge flat-panel television was positioned above a fireplace in the center of the room and the wall on the left was again made of windows.. A sofa and armchairs created a seating area that just begged to be enjoyed. Bookcases covered the opposite wall and were filled completely.

The bedroom was located on the other side of the wall with the double-sided fireplace serving both rooms. The huge four-poster bed was made of rich cherry and was covered with a relaxed-looking light-blue comforter and adorned with pillows. Claire was happy to see that Jason hadn't made his bed. Somehow that made him seem more human. While the rest of the home had a casual elegance, the bedroom and the sitting room decor felt truly comfortable and homey.

"You missed your calling. Why aren't you an architect? You could certainly be very successful, because this house is amazing. It's simply beautiful," she enthused.

He looked very happy and relieved at her statement. "I'm so happy you like it. I want you to feel at ease here."

Coming over to take her hand, Jason said, "Claire, if you feel like you need some space, you are more than welcome to use the guestroom. I would like you here with me, in my bed. But I'm not going to pressure you. It's completely your decision and I'll respect it."

Touched by the sincerity in his voice, she reached up and pulled his head to hers, lowering her lips softly against his for a brief kiss. "I want to be with you. I need to be near you tonight."

He pulled her tightly against him, her head resting

on his shoulder. "I need it too. I just want to feel you in my arms, no pressure to make love. I'm going to get our suitcases out of the car. I wouldn't mind having a quick shower before dinner and you might feel the same way. If you want to take the master bath, I'll use the one upstairs."

He gave her a kiss on the forehead then released her and pointed toward the bathroom door. The master bath was as beautiful as the rest of the house. A huge marble whirlpool tub dominated one corner of the room with a separate shower stall, and a double sink with a granite-topped vanity. She wrinkled her nose as she inspected her appearance. She looked pale, tired, and rumpled. A hot shower was just what she needed to feel human again.

She stripped off and slid into the shower. She sighed in pleasure as the spray of the water eased some of the tension in her shoulders. She reached for Jason's shampoo and lathered her hair and rinsed. Twenty minutes later, she felt like a different person. She located a hair dryer under the vanity and was soon looking for her suitcase. She found that Jason had left it right outside the door for her. The only nightgown she'd packed was a bit dressy, but she didn't feel like changing back into clothes. She pulled the long, lilac silk gown over her head, grateful she'd thought to pack the matching robe as well. She belted it tightly around her waist and then pulled a hair clip from her bag and secured her hair in a loose knot at the nape of her neck.

She opened the bedroom door and was met with the smell of something delicious. She followed her nose to the kitchen and found Jason at the stove with a kitchen towel thrown over his shoulder and a frying pan in his hand. He had also opted for something casual and wore a pair of low-riding blue lounge pants and a South Carolina Gamecocks T-shirt.

She'd seen Jason in expensive suits and in jeans, but this was the look that seemed to suit him best. He didn't look like a rich business owner even with the opulent surroundings. He simply looked like someone you could depend on, someone you could love. *Whoaaaa, girl! Where did that come from? You sleep with a guy a couple of times, and suddenly you're picking out china and writing his name on your notebook?*

Fatigue had apparently affected her more than she realized. She was feeling fragile and entirely too needy where he was concerned. It was hard to remember that twenty-four hours ago she had been livid at him, ready to pack her bags and never look back. As if by mutual agreement, that subject hadn't been brought up, even though Claire knew it was just on hold and not forgotten.

He had been wonderful today, and his support had felt so good. She rarely had anyone to lean on anymore. She did have Suzy, who would do anything for her, but somehow it wasn't the same. The issues with Jason were far from over and had to be addressed as soon as she had the strength to do it. For now, there was comfort in this moment, pretending that someone loved her.

"I hope you like omelets. It's the specialty of the house."

"I love them. It sounds wonderful. I'm impressed at how at home you seem in the kitchen."

"Don't be too impressed—I've got limited abilities. After a while, it gets very old to eat out every night. I'm not going to lie—I do have a housekeeper who comes in a couple of times a week and takes care of the grocery shopping and cleaning. If left to my own devices, there would probably be nothing but chips and beer in the kitchen and dirty clothes trickling through the doorways."

He set two plates and glasses in front of the bar stools at the island along with orange juice. She poured them both a glass of juice and walked over to the window to look out at the dark ocean. "You must love being able to see this view from almost every room in the house. It's so relaxing."

With a smile, he said, "I've always loved the ocean. It's one of the reasons I've never moved Danvers, even though there have been many offers and opportunities. We'd probably grow faster located elsewhere, but I couldn't bring myself to leave this area. It's home. Charleston is a great place and I enjoyed growing up there, but Myrtle Beach is where my heart is."

He slid a delicious-looking omelet onto her plate. Drinking her juice, she waited for him to finish making his omelet so that they could eat together. A few moments later, he was settled in next to her, and she dug in as if she were starving. She was embarrassed to find that she'd completely cleaned her plate, and he was watching her with an amused expression in his beautiful blue eyes. "Guess I was hungrier than I realized."

"You have barely had anything to eat today. Would you like me to make you another one?"

"Oh no, I'm full now. You're a great cook." He finished his own and took their plates to the dishwasher. Looking at the wall clock, she was surprised to see that it was almost midnight. As if on cue, a big yawn escaped her mouth as fatigue firmly settled in. Jason took her hand and used his other to switch off the lights as they walked back to the bedroom.

He stripped off his shirt but left his lounge pants on. She went into the bathroom to brush her teeth and left her robe on the hook next to his. He took his turn in the bathroom, and she climbed into the bed on the side he indicated. With another yawn, she closed her eyes to rest for a few minutes until he returned.

Suddenly she felt an arm going around her, and she was being pulled against a hard chest, her head resting in the crook of Jason's shoulder. She allowed herself to melt against him and soon settled into a dreamless sleep, secure in the strong arms that held her through the night.

Sometime later, as the sun was just starting to rise over the ocean, Jason turned her in his arms and made slow, mind-blowing love to her. Every time they were to-gether seemed to burn hotter than the last. He brought her to heights that she'd never dreamed existed. After collapsing against him in complete satisfaction, she felt his warm mouth against her forehead. His hands stroked her back and hair with such tenderness, it brought tears to her eyes.

"Honey, I hate to, but I have to go into the office for a while this morning. I'm going to call a car to pick me up so that you may use mine today. Do you think you know the way to the hospital from here?"

"I . . . I'm not sure. Can you leave me some direc-tions?"

"Of course. I'll write them down and leave them in the kitchen. Make yourself at home. Anything I have is yours. I'll come to the hospital when I can get free, but if you need me at all just call, okay?"

After another kiss, he quickly showered and dressed. As soon as he was gone, she called the hospital and was told that her mother's doctor would be making his rounds at nine. She quickly dressed and found the di-rections in the kitchen along with a beautiful flower that she suspected he had pulled from the front flower bed. Claire inhaled its sweet fragrance and then grabbed her purse, along with the directions that he had left. She locked the door behind her and settled into Jason's Mercedes.

The difference between his car and her poor Toyota was like night and day. Even though Daisy was dependable, she'd lost her beauty long ago and luxury was never part of the package. The seats in Jason's car were buttery soft and all the gadgets made her wish she had time to explore each of them. She easily followed his directions, and the hospital was indeed not far from his home. Claire hoped and prayed that the doctor would have encouraging news for her today.

Chapter Twenty-three

When Claire entered the ICU wing of the hospital, she spotted her mother's nurse, Glenda, at the nurses' station. Glenda looked up as she approached and gave her a warm smile. "Good morning, Ms. Walters. How are you today?"

"Good morning, Glenda. I'm good. How are you?"

"I'm busy, busy as usual, but I wouldn't have it any other way. Your mother had a good, restful night and is awake this morning. She's confused as to what's happened to her and where she is, which is normal. I think she'll be relieved to see a familiar face." Glenda came around the corner of the nurses' station and pulled her to the side. "Dr. Mauldin will be around soon and will discuss the specifics of your mother's case with you. I want to prepare you for what I've noticed this morning when checking on her. Your mother has obvious speech difficulty. There's some drooping evident on her face and also some problems gripping with her left hand. Now this isn't unusual with a stroke, and I'm not trying to scare you; I just wanted you to be prepared so that you don't panic in front of your mother."

Claire swallowed hard and drew a deep breath. "Thank you Glenda. I really appreciate you letting me know." With a motherly pat on the shoulder, Glenda went back to the nurse's station, and Claire put on a brave face and entered her mother's room.

Her mother's eyes were closed and she appeared to be resting. Claire studied her intently, looking for signs of what Glenda had mentioned. Her mother appeared perfectly normal in sleep, so peaceful that it was hard to believe she'd had a recent stroke. She pulled a chair up to the side of the bed and gently reached over to take her hand. Had she ever really noticed how beautiful her mother was?

With so many years spent with an overbearing husband who dominated a room, her mother had faded into the background. She now realized that this was her way of coping and also of protecting herself from his wrath. When she thought back through the years, Claire found it hard to remember one instance where she knew what her mother was wearing or how she looked.

All those years living with him had literally made her into a ghost who barely existed against the backdrop of his constant anger and ridicule. She had so little time to recover after he had died before she was stricken with Alzheimer's. In the end, Claire felt that not only had he broken her spirit long ago; he had also broken her mind. Really seeing her today for the first time, she wept inside for the beautiful person both inside and out who had never been strong enough to make the break that she needed to survive.

Maybe part of her should feel anger toward her mother for not leaving her father and taking them away from the abuse they'd all endured for so long. Now Claire understood that her mother simply had not been strong enough to survive the fallout that would have caused. Thoughts of Jason surfaced as she thought of the liberties he had taken with her life without consulting her. Did her father start out that way, taking over areas of her mother's life until he controlled every aspect of it? A sick feeling settled in the pit of her stomach. Would looking at her mother soon be like looking in a mirror?

A knock sounded at the door and a handsome older man in blue scrubs and a white lab coat walked into the room. With a hand extended toward Claire he said, "I'm Dr. Mauldin, and I'll be handling your mother's care while she's here." She shook his hand and introduced herself. He walked to the bedside and studied the chart he had brought in with him.

"I understand your mother rested well last night but appears to be showing some stroke-related symptoms. There are times when the stroke is mild and very minor, when temporary symptoms are detected. Other times, when the stroke is more severe, symptoms are greater and long-term or permanent. Where your mother will end up in this scenario, only time will tell. Even though it's still early in this process, I would put your mother closer to the moderate-to-severe category."

"Does that mean she won't improve?"

"Of course not, but what it does mean is that the road will be longer and the need for rehabilitation much greater. It's possible the damage could be less severe than I predict, but based on her symptoms thus far, you need to be prepared for what lies ahead."

Claire felt what hope she had slowly start to die. The look on Dr. Mauldin's face clearly showed the gravity of the situation. At that moment, she felt her mother's hand move on her own as her eyes opened, and she slowly looked around the room. Claire forced a smile on her face as her mother focused on her. "Ch . . . Ch . . . ris. . . ." Her heart fell. It wasn't unusual for her mother to mistake her for her dead sister. It was the apparent struggle of her trying to form the word that was the most heartbreaking. The terror and frustration were evident in her eyes as she looked at Claire.

Dr. Mauldin stepped forward and took her mother's arm. "Mrs. Walters, I'm Dr. Mauldin, and you're in the hospital. You had a stroke yesterday and were brought here. I know you're confused right now and probably a little scared. We're going to take care of you. Just take your time when trying to speak or move for a bit. A stroke can make things more difficult for a while and what's normally so easy may be harder." He continued on in a patient, soothing voice. "We're going to run some tests on you in the next few days. You will get so sick of seeing me that you will be trying to lock me out, but we're going to be a great team, you and I. I'm stopping all previous medications except for the insulin, and we will slowly see what needs to be added back or changed. You will tell me what you're feeling and what you need, and I'll do my best to make it happen. I work right here in this hospital, so if you need me anytime, you have one of the nurses give me a call. I take care of my own and you're one of them now, okay?"

Claire was moved at the obvious genuineness in Dr. Mauldin's voice. She could tell that her mother was also soothed by his promises, and some of the panic eased out of her eyes. "Now, I'm going to go set up some tests for later this morning and let you and your daughter have a chance to visit. If it's okay, I'll call you Evelyn from this point; we're going to be good friends before this is over." Her mother nodded in agreement and Dr. Mauldin left them alone.

She looked down at her mother and said, "Mom, you're going to be okay. I know you're scared but please believe we will get you the help you need."

Tears started to flow from her mother's eyes as she said, "Cl . . . ai . . . re."

Somehow just hearing her mother managing to say her name after several attempts was one of the sweetest and saddest moments of her life. "Mom, please just try to rest now and build your strength back up. You heard

Dr. Mauldin say they're doing tests today, so they'll know how best to help you."

"Soo . . . rr . . . y. . . . n . . . ot . . . g . . . ood . . . mo . . . m."

It took her a few seconds to figure out what her mother was trying to say to her. "Mom! Why would you say that? This isn't your fault and it sure doesn't make you a bad mother. I love you very much, and your being sick will never change that."

As her own tears began to flow despite her best efforts to hold them back, she reached down to brush the tears away from her mother's cheeks.

"Di . . . d . . . no . . . t . . . s . . . av . . . e . . . my . . . baa . . . bie . . . s." In that moment she knew exactly what she was referring to. Even after he was gone, the presence of her father lingered heavily in the room, alive in Claire and her mother's memories.

The abuse Claire received at the hands of her father would never leave her, but she'd managed to make a life for herself. Her mother, however, had never really had that reprieve. She moved from the prison of living with an abusive husband to the prison of Alzheimer's and now those walls were once again closing in around her. Regret and something close to shame were clearly reflected in the depths of her eyes.

"Mom, the past is over. Daddy made you a prisoner, but now you're free and you deserve to be happy and enjoy your life. I realize that you spent most of your life trying to deflect his anger onto you and away from us." She leaned down and put her arms around her mother as best she could, and they stayed like that until the door opened.

"Can anyone join in this hug?"

Claire saw Louise smiling in the doorway and held out a hand to her. "Group hug, then." She insisted that Louise take the one chair in the room, and she stood near the window. "How did you get here this morning? I was going to call and see if you wanted me to pick you up."

"My sister dropped me on her way to play bingo," Louise said and laughed. "You know nothing can keep her from getting in there and hoping for the big payoff."

She noticed her mother looked much better once Louise arrived. She'd been part of their lives for so long that she was like a sister—and maybe a bit of a mother—to them both. Claire could tell that Louise brought the same calming influence to her mother that she always did. Soon Evelyn was trying to smile along with them as they joked and tried to lighten the mood.

Glenda arrived around eleven and wheeled her mother off for her first round of tests. Louise said she was going to the restroom and to stretch her legs for a bit. Claire decided to go to the waiting room and find some magazines to pass the time. She neared the nurses' station and was surprised to see Jason deep in conversation with Dr. Mauldin.

He spotted her and walked over to give her a hug. "Hi there, how is your mom doing today?"

"Umm, pretty good. When did you get here?"

"A few moments ago. I met Tom on my way in, and we were catching up. We both serve on some of the same charities and have known each other for years. Your mother couldn't be in better hands. I told Tom that your mother was to have whatever she needs, so don't worry about anything."

She felt her spine stiffen. She gave Dr. Mauldin a tight smile and turned to Jason. "May I talk to you privately for a minute?"

Obviously puzzled by her behavior, Jason replied, "Sure. Tom, it was great to see you again. I'm sure we will talk soon."

Jason steered her down the hall and stepped out a side door into a small courtyard. When he attempted to put his arms around her, she stiffened and pushed away. "Jason, why were you discussing my mother's medical care with her doctor?"

Still looking confused, he said, "As I mentioned, Tom and I are friends, and I wanted him to know that your mother could afford to have any care that she might need. Doctors have their hands tied these days getting insurance companies to approve adequate care for their patients, and I don't want this to be the case with your mother. I know how important she is to you."

"Jason, I appreciate the fact that you care, but I need to make these decisions. I realize that you're somewhat in the know about my mother's financial situation, but

I must be completely informed so that I can make the necessary judgments concerning her care. I can't promise the hospital or the doctor that I can give them a blank check for whatever they deem necessary. We're not rich. I can, however, start making arrangements as soon as the doctor discusses options with *me*."

"Honey, you don't have to worry about looking at options. I'm perfectly happy to pay for whatever your mother might need. You don't need the additional stress of thinking about money while you're worrying about your mother. I've got the money and I would like nothing better than to help you. I'm not trying to take over here, but I do want your mother to have every opportunity to recover."

"I know that you feel like you're helping, and I do appreciate it, but she's my mother, and I need to make the decisions. Please let me handle this, and I would appreciate it if you'd not discuss my mother's case with her doctor without my knowledge."

He was temporarily at a loss for words. "Claire, I've obviously upset you, which was not my intention. Tom asked me who I was seeing at the hospital, which brought up the subject of your mother. As I said, I know how important she is to you and I wanted to make sure you didn't have to worry about her getting the help that she needs. I'm sorry if I've upset you. I'll of course respect your wishes in this." She stared into his eyes and saw nothing but sincerity.

Was she overreacting? Was her past relationship

with her father coloring everything she did? Still feeling uneasy despite his assurances, she knew that the hospital was probably not the best place for a heart-to-heart talk with him and decided to let the matter drop for now. Soon, though, they had to discuss his habit of trying to run her life. He had to understand that she was capable of making her own decisions. Maybe her mother and father started out this way in the beginning, and then he started taking over small areas of her mother's life until he finally consumed her?

Boy, he royally messed this one up. His conversation with Tom had started innocently, as he had indicated to Claire. His assurance to Tom that he wanted the best for her mother, regardless of the cost, had gone a little beyond what he had admitted to her. Taking care of people was second nature to him. He never considered himself a nurturing person; he was simply someone who saw a problem or a need and fixed it.

One thing having money—and plenty of it—had taught him was that most everything could be fixed for a price. He wasn't consumed by money and didn't throw it around. He did, however, appreciate the good deeds that he could easily do because of it. Growing up as he had obviously colored his views of relationships. Whatever he had with Claire now was the closest he had ever been to a committed relationship, and he was committed to her, more than she would be comfortable knowing.

He needed her. He burned for her, and he longed for the taste of her. He stayed in an almost constant start of arousal now. If she walked into the room, he was hard within minutes. Each time he thought he had sated his hunger for her, but it only burned brighter. She was a witch, and he was completely under her spell. It wasn't just the sex though that held him spellbound; it was Claire.

He loved that she worried about everyone around her, but never herself. He loved how she sucked her lower lip into her mouth when she was deep in thought, he loved how his house had felt like a home with her inside, and he loved her independence even though he didn't know how to handle it and seemed to screw up at every turn.

How could you explain to someone that, basically, you were born to take care of people? He often thought his mother had decided to have a child simply to have someone to solve all her problems at any time of the day or night. He had never been a child, though; he had been the go-to man since he was old enough to walk and talk. Hell, he still spent a good part of his time solving his mother's problems.

After almost losing Claire over the loan at work and the loss of her job at Partiez Plus, he told himself he would not interfere in her life again, but he had stumbled today. His need to protect her was taking over with little thought to the consequences. Being involved with someone who seemed to want nothing from him other than, well, *him* was something new, and frankly, he didn't know how to act. He was a smart man. Surely he could manage to keep it together enough not to ruin the best thing to happen to him.

Claire walked Jason to the exit door of the hospital, where his car was waiting. He rarely used a car and driver even though someone in his position could easily afford to. He had assured her that he didn't need his Mercedes and wanted her to keep it. Even though she was still uneasy over their earlier conversation, she promised she was going to run by her apartment that evening to pick up a few things and would return to his house to stay for the night.

Maybe that wasn't the best idea; she felt like she needed time to think about her relationship with him. Things seemed to have moved so far, so fast. She would take some extra time this evening when she was at her apartment to think.

Dr. Mauldin made his last round of the day and indicated he would have the test results sometime tomorrow. Her mother was going to start some light rehabilitation to keep up her muscle tone. She was having great difficulty forming her words and with using of her left arm and hand. Louise's sister had picked her up a few minutes ago and Claire was preparing to leave since visiting hours ended soon.

They'd given her mother a light sleeping pill to help her anxiety and ensure she rested well. Her mother seemed to be less confused this afternoon, and Claire was grateful for the patient, encouraging manner of Dr. Mauldin and Glenda. Claire knew they were just getting started on a long road, but today, at least, she felt somewhat encouraged that there could be a light somewhere at the end of the tunnel.

Chapter Twenty-four

Claire pulled the Mercedes beside her Toyota in front of her apartment. Luckily each apartment was assigned two spaces, which she rarely needed. As she was getting out of the car, she saw Billy approaching from the other side. With an inward groan, she tried to plaster on a friendly smile. "Hey, Billy, how have you been?"

"Hey, Claire, no complaints. I'm doing good. Where is your boyfriend?"

"Oh, I'm just picking up a few things. He isn't along this time." *Ugh, great, Claire, why don't you ask him to abduct you next since you admitted to being alone?* "He's waiting for me, though, so I need to run in and pick up a few things and be on my way."

"Are you moving in with him?"

"Oh, I don't know; we haven't made any decisions on that yet."

"Claire, I just wanted to say I was sorry if I scared you before, you know, when I kept asking you out. I admit, Billy did have kind of a crush on you, and I hoped we could get together, but since your boyfriend came and talked to me and told me how I was scaring you, well, old Billy was just embarrassed."

She was trying not to smile at Billy's continued use of himself in the third person when his words started to sink in. "What're you talking about Billy? When did you talk to Jason?"

"Well, I guess it was the next day after I met you two here. He came to see me and told me I was making you uncomfortable. He was real nice but serious, you know, trying to protect his girl. Billy can respect that, being a man and all. Don't you worry at all about your place while you're gone. I'll keep an eye on things." Somehow managing to say something in parting to Billy, she stumbled into her apartment and closed the door.

My God, Jason really has taken over my entire life. What other things were there that she didn't know? Had he contacted everyone she knew to cut her off from the world, just like her father did to her mother? She walked into her bedroom and collapsed on the bed, all the hope that he was different going out of her.

The signs had all been there; she'd just chosen to ignore them. It felt so good to have someone in her life that genuinely seemed to care about her, someone to lean on for the first time in her life. This was a side of Jason that was completely unexpected. Sure, he was dominating in business, but most successful men were. He cared about everyone in the company—that much was obvious.

To be involved with him, though, was to lose her identity, and then how long after would the abuse start? Her father hadn't always been someone her mother considered a monster. She probably felt protected and cherished at first until he slowly chipped away at everything she was. Even though Claire's heart was breaking, it was time to walk away from him while she still had the strength to do it.

She didn't know how long she'd been lying in the dark when she heard a knock at the door. *Oh wonderful, Billy has some more bad news for me. Maybe Jason kicked his dog after threatening him.* Wearily getting to her feet, she walked to the door and swung it open without checking to see who was on the other side.

Jason stood there, a warm smile on his face. He stepped forward to kiss her lightly on the lips and then walked around her into the apartment, seeming not to notice the frozen expression on her face. "I had my driver drop me here. I thought I could help you pack some of your things, and we could stop for dinner on the way home." Suddenly he stopped to examine her face and the rumpled condition of her clothing. "Were you resting?"

"Jason, I'm not going to your house tonight." She walked over to the side table where she had tossed his keys and handed them to him.

"What's going on? You want to stay here? I guess I could grab a few things from home and come back if that's what you really want."

She tried to draw on her earlier anger to keep the tears in check and said, "I don't want you here, either. Whatever this is that we've been doing is over. I know this will make working together impossible, so I'll find another job. Suzy can pick my things up for me at the office."

"Whoa! What the hell are you talking about? I seem to have missed out on something major here. You're breaking up with me because I talked to your mother's doctor today? I know I might have been out of line a bit, but I don't think that's any reason to take this drastic step."

She could see the confusion in his eyes and the red flush covering his face. His normal unflappable cool seemed to be deserting him. "It's not just that, Jason, but it's a series of things like that. This is best for the both of us. I've been controlled almost my entire life. I can't make the mistake of continuing the cycle."

"You're upset over your mother, and you're overreacting. Let's talk about our relationship later when you have calmed down some," he said in a soothing voice.

She saw red at the patronizing tone of his voice. Anger took control as she yelled, "Don't talk to me like I'm an idiot, Jason. I know exactly what I'm doing, and as for our relationship, we don't have one! We slept together a few times, but great sex doesn't mean we're married now!"

She sucked in a breath and prepared to deliver the final blow, knowing she was going to have to twist the knife even deeper to get him to leave. "I tried, Jason, I really did, but you just aren't my type. I've been seeing someone else that I met at one of the bachelor parties, and I think we're a better fit. I'm not looking for anything serious, and you're smothering me," she finished with a pitying smile.

He stared at her like he had never seen her before. His handsome face went white, completely devoid of color. With a look of pure disgust, he spun on his heel and slammed her door without uttering a single word in response.

On shaky legs, she walked over and locked her door and collapsed on the floor. Sobs ripped from her throat as every piece of her heart shattered into a million pieces. She knew that as long as she lived, she would never be whole again. She loved him. The lust that she'd always joked with herself about feeling for him had been love all along. Just knowing she would never see him at the office, never see those blue eyes twinkle when he laughed, never feel his hands on her body bringing her to a frenzied pitch made her want to run after him and beg him to forgive her, but she couldn't.

In ten years or less, she would be her mother and she would rather be alone than love someone so bent on consuming her. As she curled up into a ball on the floor, Claire wondered if she would ever find the strength or will to move again.

Jason walked to his car in disbelief. He wanted to turn around, go back and demand to know what was going on, but the memory of the cold, remote expression on Claire's face stopped him. Had the things that he thought he was doing to help her been the very things that were pushing her away? He didn't believe the bit about her seeing someone else. That just wasn't the way she was made. He knew it was his actions alone that had pushed her away and, for that, he had no answer.

Ironic, really, that the one time in his life that he let himself depend on another person, get emotionally involved, he was kicked in the stomach and discarded like yesterday's trash. If this was how love made you feel, then he was finished with it. Almost on autopilot, he arrived home and entered a house that had seemed to be filled with such promise only this morning.

Chapter Twenty-five

Claire somehow survived the next week. Most of her mother's test results were back, and the news wasn't as promising as she'd hoped but not a worst-case scenario either. Dr. Mauldin didn't feel that another stroke was imminent. The damage sustained from this one was more than likely permanent, and her mother would need months of rehabilitation to learn to cope with the handicaps left behind.

The process would be slow with her Alzheimer's. Dr. Mauldin was convinced that her mother would need to move into a rehabilitation center for a while rather than trying it on an outpatient basis. Her insurance would cover some of the cost but would still leave a large amount that needed to be paid. She walked back out into the waiting room and put her face in her hands. How was she going to cover all the expenses?

She felt a touch on her head and looked up into the concerned eyes of Louise. Louise took one of her hands and said, "Honey, I know you're overwhelmed and trying to decide what to do. If you don't mind an old woman giving you some advice, I would like to tell you something that you don't know."

Her curiosity piqued, Claire waited for her to continue. "Many years ago there were two old women who liked to think ahead. In a house where it wasn't encouraged to think at all, much less make any plans, we did what we could on our own. Your mama always knew you were the strong one. Even back then she sensed at some point you'd be taking care of us all. Your daddy moved everything into your mama's name well before he died. He claimed it was for tax purposes, but I really believe he just wanted to be free and clear, in case he decided to run off with one of those floozies that he loved to hang out with."

Almost choking in surprise, she said, "Floozies?"

"Honey, there isn't another word for them, and I think you always knew your daddy liked the women. He wanted your mama under his thumb as the status symbol of the happily married man, but he also wanted the wild ones to run with. We told your daddy many times that we were going to the market or some errand, but actually we were meeting my cousin Bill, a lawyer we could trust. Your mama had everything, including the house, put into your name years ago. We were really careful to keep it hidden. Your daddy never thought anyone had a brain other than him, so he never really looked hard enough to find out. Honey, that house is worth a lot of money. It may be in disrepair, but it's on prime land and would bring a pretty penny if you sold it. I know you think your mama would never adjust if she left there, but it's the opposite really. It's taken me a long time to realize it, but that house has been her prison for so long, she needs to get out. There are so many bad memories there for her that I think she hides inside her mind just to escape them."

Claire could feel her mouth opening and closing with no sounds coming out. "My God, Louise, I had no idea! Why would she put the house in my name with Chrissie still alive?"

"Honey, we both know your sister wasn't very strong. Now, your mama had no idea what would happen to her; she just took steps to protect you girls. She wanted you to be able to sell the house and have the money to take care of you and your sister. She held on there so many years to give that to you."

Tears were rolling down her face as she gripped Louise's hand tightly. "I never knew. I thought she was completely in denial over what was going on. I can't believe you two did all of this on your own and managed to hide it from him. That took a lot of guts."

Louise smiled at her and laughed. "Honey, us old ladies still got a trick or two up our sleeves. Now, you find someone to list that house with and set your mama free. She needs a new life and so do you. It's time all those ghosts were laid to rest. Someone else can come in and make a life there and give that place some happy memories."

*   *   *

Claire talked to her mother that afternoon about everything Louise had told her. She saw a sparkle in her mother's eyes that had never been there before, and it looked strangely like pride. It was a strain for her mother to talk, but she managed to confirm her wishes for the house to be sold.

Claire spent the afternoon arranging for a real estate agent to meet her there the next day. She also called an employment agency and lined up some interviews at the end of the week. If she could find an office job during the day, she could also work a weekend job when her mother was settled into the rehabilitation center.

She took a few moments to check the messages on her cell phone, which she'd been ignoring. Julie had left several messages wanting to know why she wasn't working for Partiez Plus any longer. Suzy had also been ringing her phone off the hook, so as soon as she was settled at home, she returned her call.

"Girlfriend, you got some explaining to do. I call and call and you never answer. Are we seeing other friends now or something?"

With a laugh, Claire said, "Nope, you know you're my one and only. It's been crazy here. I've almost lived at the hospital. Thank you for the flowers that you brought to Mom; she really loved them. She's the envy of everyone on the floor now."

"I'm glad she liked them. I'm sorry I missed you

when I dropped by. I thought I could grill you, um, I mean, feed you."

"Grill me, huh? About what?"

With a long, dramatic sigh, Suzy said, "Don't act dumb, babe. It's so not you. I know that your love life has hit the skids for some reason. From the looks of Jason, I don't think it's his idea. The man looks like he has been run over by a truck. Candace, who has been filling in for you, says he never leaves the office. He's there when she gets there and there when she leaves. She suspects he has been sleeping there. I'm even starting to question his bathing habits, ugh. So what gives with you two? And before you even say it, I know I'm nosey as hell but, hey, it's part of my charm, right? You seemed so happy with him, so what happened?"

"Oh, Suz, I wanted him to be something he wasn't."

"And what was that?"

"I wanted him to be the man of my dreams, not the man of my nightmares."

"Babe, I don't get it—was he into freaky stuff or something? He sure doesn't look like the type, though he does look yummy."

"Um, Suz, earth to Suz, come back now. What I mean is he's just like my father." Suzy was quiet for so long, she wondered if she was still there. Over a bottle of wine one evening, she'd told Suzy all about her years of abuse at the hands of her father.

"Why would you think that?"

"Remember when I told you Jason tried to loan me money and the fight we had over it? You explained to me that he had helped several people you knew."

"Yeah, so you're still mad about that?"

"No, other things have happened. Things I can't get over."

She went on to tell her about the papers she'd found in his briefcase while they were in Charleston, about the incident at the hospital, and what Billy had told her.

When she was finished Suzy for once was actually speechless. "Wow, he has been a busy boy, hasn't he? He's like a fairy godmother or something, isn't he?"

"You see, don't you? He's everything I've been running away from my whole life. I had to get away, make the break before it was too late."

"Claire, I know you haven't had an easy life. Hell, it has pretty much raised its leg and peed right on you. Jason has, for sure, lost control there a bit, no doubt. Actually, a little bat-shit crazy on the giving money away for free, but I already thought that. Sweetie, I don't think he's anything like your father. I know he's scaring you by trying to take care of all of your needs before you even know you have them, but I'm telling you, the man has a good heart. Can you honestly say there was an instance when you felt like your father had a good heart? Did you ever feel like he was trying to protect you and care for you?"

"No, but, Suz, you don't know how my father started off. Abusive people usually escalate over time.

They probably don't just go off the deep end immediately. We'd only been together for a short time and really not even in a relationship and look at how he had taken over my life. What would it be like in a month or a year? Would I even recognize myself then?" She felt a sob escape from her throat and fought for calm.

Suzy, as if sensing how close Claire was to losing it, took a quieter tone, all joking gone from her voice. "Sweetie, do you know what I think you need to do? I think you need to talk to the one person who can tell you how things started off with your father, your mother. You're still hurting and traumatized from everything you and your family suffered. It would probably do your mother some good to get it out as well."

"I can't. She isn't up to talking about this, and I can't risk upsetting her."

"Sweetie, did you ever stop to think that your mother needs it as much as you do? You have spent these last few years since your father and sister died trying to pretend that nothing bad happened. It's so bottled up inside you that you're ready to explode. Give your mother a chance to be your mom and to be strong for you for once. Go talk to her before you throw away your chance with Jason."

"I . . . I'll think about it, Suz; I will."

"Good, because I don't have many more inspirational talks left in me. I'm practically breaking out in hives right now."

Despite herself, Claire laughed long and hard. She

loved that Suzy always knew when to throw in some comic relief.

"Okay, girl, I gotta run. Love you and all that stuff." With a click, she was gone.

That was Suzy—in like a tornado, out like a tornado.

Chapter Twenty-six

Claire tossed and turned all night, going over and over what Suzy had said. Could she be right about Jason? Was there a good man under the take-charge exterior? Suzy was right. There was only one person who could set her mind at ease. She desperately wanted to talk to her mother, but maybe Louise was a good starting point. Louise's sister usually dropped her off for the day around nine, so Claire rushed to catch her for a cup of coffee before she talked to her mother.

She arrived a little earlier than usual and checked with Glenda at the nurses' station. Her mother rested well and was on her way to morning therapy. Glenda also said that Louise hadn't arrived yet. She thanked her and walked to the front entrance to wait for her. In a few moments, she saw a long blue Cadillac pulling in front of the circular drive and Louise getting out of the passenger side. She shuddered as the Cadillac took off at a fast clip. She could easily imagine Louise hanging on for dear life as her sister sped through the city.

Louise looked surprised but pleased to see her standing inside the doorway. Louise said, "It's good to see you smiling this morning, honey. You have been so quiet this week."

"I know, Louise. There's been a lot to take in lately, and I'm just now catching my breath. Mom just went down for her physical therapy, so I thought we could have a cup of coffee, if you like?" There was a small coffee shop located in the hospital that served coffee, cappuccinos, and various pastries. They both chose a regular coffee and fresh hot cinnamon rolls before settling in at a table in the back of the room. The shop was a revolving door of doctors and nurses getting their morning fill of caffeine to start their day.

"Louise, I know we haven't talked about it, but what're your plans if we sell the house? You're more than welcome to stay with me. My apartment is on the small side, but I would be happy to have you there," she offered.

"You're a sweet child to worry about this old woman but don't. My sister, Janet, and I've talked, and I plan to move in with her. Her husband has been gone for a long time now. She stays busy with her senior group and bingo, but she's lonely in the house by herself. She's already agreed to bring me to visit Evelyn as often as I want, and we get along well. I want you to promise to come see me though, honey. I never had children. I didn't need them. You and Chrissie were always my babies."

Claire felt tears gather in her eyes. For someone who never cried, she never seemed to stop now. "I promise

I will, and you know I think of you as a mother as well." When they'd both gotten themselves somewhat under control, she looked at Louise and said, "I wanted to talk to you about my father. I know you weren't there in the beginning, but I want to know if you ever saw any good in him."

Louise looked at her in surprise, sadness etched in the corners of her mouth. "Honey, I wondered when or if you'd ever be strong enough to ask about him. I know we've mentioned him plenty, but we never really talked about him. Your mama and I did, though, quite a lot. I think it helped her to have an outlet for her anger. Once I asked your mama almost the same question; you know, was he good to her in the beginning and when did it change.

"You know they met in college. Your mama said she was quiet and shy back then, kind of a wallflower. Even though we both know from the pictures she was beautiful, and still is, she was always more involved in her studies than dating. When your daddy started paying attention to her, she was flattered. All the girls in school were chasing him, and it made her feel special to have someone like him chasing her.

"She started going out with him, and even though she caught him talking to other girls a lot, he always had an excuse. By that time, she was so in love with him she believed every word he said. He would insult her in front of his friends to embarrass her and then beg her to forgive him later. He always found a way to make it her fault. She caught him quite literally with his pants down with the captain of the cheerleading squad after they'd been going out for a year. He told her it just happened because he didn't think she loved him enough, and he was afraid she would leave him. He proposed right there on the spot and your mama, the innocent that she was, believed him.

"Your daddy used love to cover his trail of lies until after they were married. She would threaten to leave him, and he would tell her he couldn't live without her. He would be good for a few weeks, and the cycle would repeat. After she had you girls, she was determined to shield you as much as she could. Your daddy told her if she ever left him, she would never see you and Chrissie again. He was a lawyer with a lot of powerful friends, and they'd never take the side of someone like her against him. She did try, Claire; she wanted out. She was so afraid of what would happen if she left.

"Her greatest fear was that you and Chrissie would be left alone with him. She always tried to make sure he burned out the worst of his anger on her so that nothing was left to be directed at you girls. I honestly think she would have killed him if he'd ever raised a hand to you. He tried his best to break her and he assumed that he had long ago. But he never did. She lived for the day you'd all be free and, when that finally happened, there was no joy in it because Chrissie had been taken. I think she always felt that by wishing for him to be gone, she was responsible for what happened to Chrissie. Honey, you both need to talk about it and then move past it. I know that young man of yours would very much like to build a life with you free of ghosts."

Claire looked at her in surprise.

"I might be an old woman, but I'm not senile. I saw the way that boy looked at you. I think you'd be surprised to hear what your mama has to say about him too. Why don't you go on back and see if she's in her room now? I'm going to have me another cup of coffee and rest for a minute."

She stood and leaned down to give Louise a hug. "I love you so much. I don't know what I would do without you."

Always strong, Louise gave a suspicious sniff, and said, "I know, now you run along and see your mama. It's long overdue."

Glenda waved at her and told her that her mother was back in her room now. Claire was happy to see how much better she was looking each day. Her speech, although still difficult, had improved some. She knew that she got frustrated when trying to get the words she needed out, but she was adjusting.

"Hey, Mom, you look pretty today. Did you have a good workout?" Her mother rolled her eyes and smiled. "Louise is here. She's having a cup of coffee before she comes in for a visit. Her sister, Janet, looks pretty scary behind the wheel of that big car of hers." She laughed. Her mother smiled again and reached over on her bedside table to get something. "Mom, what's that?"

Her mother tapped her fingers on the front of it, and suddenly a voice said, "A computer." Still confused, she walked around to watch her.

Since her right hand and arm hadn't been affected by the stroke, she could type on it. Claire looked at a big keyboard made on a screen that looked like a large tablet computer. "Mom, that's amazing. Where did you get it?"

With a hesitant look, her mother typed "Jason." Shocked, she could only stare at her mother.

"My Jason?"

Instead of typing her mother said, "Y . . . es. Yo . . . ur Ja . . . son."

She sat down heavily in the chair beside the bed. "How?"

Her mother turned back to the computer and typed "He comes to see me." Just when she thought there were no more surprises where Jason was concerned, Claire was completely floored.

"Mom, when does he come to see you? I'm here all the time."

With more taps on the keypad, her mother said, "When you take Louise home."

"Just once?"

Almost reluctantly, she said, "Every evening." More typing followed. "He's a good man and he loves you." She felt like she was in the twilight zone. Her mother, who on a good day seemed out of it, was talking to her via a computer from Jason. The same Jason that Claire had thrown out of her apartment last week. Jason was now apparently visiting her mother in the hospital every evening, even though Claire had never introduced them. Had the entire world gone insane?

"Mom, um, I'm at a loss here. Why would he be visiting you and how does he know I'm not here?" Suddenly, her mother looked at her with a bright smile and started laughing. She rushed to the bedside, fearing she was having another stroke. "Mom, calm down, this isn't good for you."

Her mother shook off her concern and typed again. "Mom now taking care of you for once. I'm not letting you lose him. I told him about your father and about your fears. My story to tell. He understands now." She'd never seen her mother look so happy and free. When most people would be terrified of what they were facing, she looked like she'd slain a dragon.

It took a long time, with her mother alternating between trying to put the words together to speak and using her new computer, but they talked about her father for the first time. The person that she thought her mother to be was so different from the reality. Her mother had spent her entire life trying to protect them and, in the end, had come close to losing herself. Having the stroke, in a way, saved her life.

Dr. Mauldin had taken her off all the Alzheimer's medications and the confusion she'd lived under the last few years was clearing. Dr. Mauldin believed that instead of having Alzheimer's, her mother was dealing with depression and anxiety due to the trauma of living with an abusive husband and then the loss of her daughter. The medications she'd been prescribed were actually keeping her from recovering. Her diabetes medication was also adjusted and the change in her mental clarity was nothing short of amazing. This was a woman Claire had only ever caught glimpses of through the years.

Her mother also told her that when Jason had visited her the first time he had just missed Claire. After that, Louise always called him when she was leaving so he could visit without upsetting her. He came each evening and read to her or just talked. Last night he had brought the computer and taught her how to use it. It was obvious from her mother's expression that she really liked him.

She knew in her heart that her mother would have never been so comfortable around a man who reminded her in the least bit of her husband. Everything that Jason had done for her, although way overboard, had been to help because he cared. He hadn't been trying to control Claire or make decisions because he didn't feel like she was competent. He simply wanted to help people. He visited her mother each night because he had a big heart, not to gain something from her. She looked at her mother and a smile formed on Claire's face.

Her mother said one word. "Go."

Chapter Twenty-seven

Claire didn't know when, or if, Jason would be home, but she was determined to sleep in her car if she had to. She didn't want to talk to him over the phone or at the office. She wanted to see him in person. She needed to see if she could salvage something after the way she'd hurt him. Yes, he shared in the blame, and if they were to have a future together, he would have to learn to step back and let her handle her life. She'd been sitting in his driveway for almost three hours. She was yawning and trying to stay awake when, around midnight, approaching headlights flooded her car.

She was parked to the side and he didn't even notice her until he was pulling into the garage. His car slammed to a halt as he stared at her car. He turned off the ignition, leaving it half outside the garage, and rushed over to her car. He opened the door and asked urgently, "Claire, what's wrong? Did something happen to your mother?"

In the dim light of the car, she could make out the

tight grooves around his mouth. His beautiful blue eyes seemed so much duller than the last time they'd been together. She reached up and ran her finger down the side of his face, feeling the familiar angles, committing it to memory once again. Jason caught her hand and shook it slightly as if afraid she was in shock. "Baby, what's going on? Talk to me!"

As if a dam had broken, tears poured from her eyes as she said, "Everything is okay. I needed to see you."

Suddenly, she could see his face take on a guarded expression. "Claire, just go home. I can't do this again."

As he started to straighten and pull away from the car, she grabbed his hand and said, "I love you, Jason."

He pulled back from her, shaking his head. "You're killing me. Please just go home."

He walked away from her toward the door in his garage, leaving his car half out of the garage. Quickly getting out of her car, she caught up with him as he was unlocking the door. "Jason," she began, "I know you have been going to see my mother every evening. I know she told you about my father." She waited for his reaction as his shoulders stiffened. As he turned slowly around, she was taken aback by the desperate sadness and longing she saw on his face.

"Claire, I'm sorry. I know now that I did everything wrong with you. By loving you so much, I turned into everything you'd ever feared. I wanted to take all your pain away, and instead I only gave you more. I drove you away, and I know you will never trust me. You will always think that I'm like him."

She put her finger to his lips to stop the flow and wrapped herself around him. He stood in her embrace, still and resistant. She gently laid her lips against his and whispered, "I love you; you're everything I ever wanted and was afraid I would never find."

Beautiful blue eyes searched hers and she couldn't miss the love pouring from them. Crushing her in his embrace, he pressed his lips against hers as they shared a tender kiss full of love and promise. Some minutes later, Jason pulled back, his breathing rapid. "I love you so much and I'm sorry for everything. Please put me out of my misery and marry me because I can't make it without you. I promise to try to control the urge to solve all your problems. I love you desperately, so please be gentle with me if I stumble occasionally."

Looking up at the man that she loved so much, she said, "I would love to marry you, but do you think we could go inside now before I rip your clothes off right here?" Never had she been pulled through a door in such record time.

Chapter Twenty-eight

One year later

Claire was smiling as she walked into her husband's arms. After a quick kiss, anxious blue eyes searched her face. She had been sick on and off for the last few weeks and unable to kick the stomach bug making its rounds. Finally Jason had insisted on her going to the doctor. Despite his protests, she went alone, assuring him that he didn't need to leave work to go with her. She knew how hard he had worked to overcome his constant need to take care of her, and she realized it had been sheer torture for him not to accompany her today.

"Baby, what did the doctor say?"

With her best serious expression, she said, "Well, he said that I should be fine ... in about eight more months, that is." Seeing the look of confusion and fear in his eyes, she took his hand and gently lowered it to her stomach.

The confusion started to clear, and his eyes lit up

with joy. Swinging her up in his arms, he said, "A baby?"

"Yep, Mr. Danvers, all that overtime you have been putting in lately, um . . . in the bedroom, has really paid off."

He rubbed her stomach gently and said, "I love you, Mrs. Danvers." He then started to leave the room. "I need to get started on planning our little one's future right away."

Mouth hanging open, she looked at him, not believing her ears. He looked back at her and started laughing. "I'm sorry, baby. I couldn't resist. I promise, no planning, unless we're both in on it."

She swatted his arm and said, "You're so bad. Now, how about we take a walk on the beach and tell our neighbors the good news?"

With his arm around her, he carefully led her down the path to the beach, as if afraid she would break. Lights twinkled from a newly built house in the distance. Soon, they were approaching the house, similar in design to their own, only a smaller version.

Jason held her hand and assisted her up onto the back deck. Through the glass door, she saw a smiling Louise coming, her mother not far off. "Hey, you two, just in time for dinner! I made a big pot of spaghetti."

She was amazed at everything that had happened in the last year. Her mother still had limited use of her left arm, but her speech had improved so much that the computer was no longer necessary to help her talk.

Since being taken off all the medication that she'd not needed in the first place, her bad days seemed to be a thing of the past. She went to a therapist weekly and, although the memories of the abuse she'd suffered would always be there, they no longer controlled her life.

Jason had offered to design and build a house for her mother and Louise. He asked them what they wanted and their answer was one just like his and Claire's except smaller. That was exactly what they got. Louise had invited Janet to live with them, too, but she had a new boyfriend and was suddenly happy living alone again. Claire's mother was glowing now and looked ten years younger.

Another person walked in from the kitchen trailing her mother. Jason stepped forward, hand extended, and said, "Tom, good to see you again. Making a lot of house calls lately, aren't you?" The older man laughed as he shook Jason's hand and gave Claire a hug. Her mother and Dr. Mauldin had grown close during her hospital time, but a relationship had started only when they met again a few months ago in the grocery store.

Like her mother, he was a widower, and they found they had many similar interests. He was now a regular visitor, and Claire suspected there might be more good news soon. Her mother made it clear, though, that no matter what happened, she and Louise were a package deal and that would never change. As they all walked into the dining room and were seated, Jason lifted

Claire's hand and kissed it. "Claire and I have some exciting news."

Every eye at the table was suddenly on her. She could feel the color starting to creep into her face.

"What is it, guys?" Her mother asked nervously. Her mother and Louise of course knew that she had been sick. Gripping Tom's hand tightly she continued. "Oh God, is something wrong, honey?"

"Now, Evelyn, just let the girl speak," Louise added.

Smiling, Claire reached into her pocket and pulled out a piece of pink cloth and a piece of blue cloth. She handed the blue to her mother and the pink to Louise. Her mother looked at the folded square in confusion, but Louise started chuckling as she unfolded her pink square. Finally her mother followed Louise's example and her lips started to quiver as she read the words on the cloth. "My heart belongs to Grandma." All at once the women were sobbing and Tom was congratulating Jason and clapping him on the back.

Looking around the table at the people she loved the most, Claire felt something unlike anything she had ever known before. For a moment it was hard to figure out exactly what it was. Finally, as she gripped her husband's hand and looked into his beautiful eyes, she had her answer: peace.

Acknowledgments

A huge thank-you to Elizabeth Humphrey—you are the best!

A special thank-you to author Elle Lothlorien, for your advice and encouragement, which made me want to finally finish my first book.

Also a big thank-you to my husband, who put up with me sitting at the computer at every opportunity and bouncing all my ideas off him each day.

Author's Note

Thank you for purchasing *Weekends Required*. I hope you enjoyed reading it as much as I enjoyed writing it. I would love to hear your comments. Please feel free to e-mail me at sydney@sydneylandon.com or visit my Web site www.sydneylandon.com for updates on future books.

About the Author

Sydney Landon is a *New York Times* and *USA Today* bestselling author. When she isn't writing, Sydney enjoys reading, swimming, and being a minivan-driving soccer mom. She lives in Greenville, South Carolina, with her family.

CONNECT ONLINE

www.sydneylandon.com
facebook.com/sydney.landonauthor
twitter.com/#!/sydneylandon1
sydneylandon.com/b2evolution/blog2.php

Continue reading for a special preview of
Sydney Landon's next Danvers book,

NOT PLANNING ON YOU

Coming in February 2013 from Signet.

"Crapple Dapple, are you kidding me?" Suzy looked at her best friend Claire in horror.

"Crapple Dapple?"

Waving her hand in a vague way, Suzy said, "Oh yeah, I'm trying to stop cursing so much at work. The new receptionist crosses herself every time I roll out a four-letter word; it's kind of creepy." Suzy gave Claire a few moments to recover from the laughter shaking her body and got back to the question she'd asked. "Claire, earth to Claire, come back."

Wiping the tears from her eyes, Claire finally composed herself enough to continue. "Um, yeah, sorry, Suz, but you heard me correctly. Gray is going to take over daily operations at Danvers for the foreseeable future and Jason prefers that he relocate here to Myrtle Beach to do that. He trusts Gray and, although he will continue on as the CEO of Danvers, Gray will step up as the president of operations."

Last year, Danvers International had become the

largest communications company in the United States when it merged with Mericom. Grayson Merimon, whom everyone called Gray, was the CEO of Mericom, which had been based in Charleston, South Carolina. Much to Suzy's chagrin, once the merger was completed, he'd been spending a lot of time at the Danvers Headquarters in Myrtle Beach. Tall, dark, and handsome—yes, he had it all. The man looked like sex on a stick, and he'd made no secret of the fact that he was very interested in her. Suzy, however, wasn't interested in Gray, or so she kept telling herself. Her high school sweetheart, the man she thought she'd be spending the rest of her life with, had cheated on her, and now men were only good for one thing. And that one thing was something she wanted to avoid in the workplace.

"It's the kid, isn't it? It hasn't even been born yet and already it's turning my life upside down," Suzy groaned.

"Well, Jason does want to be able to spend more time with me and the baby when it's born so, yes, that has something to do with it."

"I knew it!" Catching herself lest she offend Claire, Suzy tried to get control. She also tried to understand why she was suddenly terrified at the thought of seeing Gray daily. She'd spent a lot of time in his company since the merger. She was always careful to have someone else present, though, when meeting with Gray. The strong, gutsy person inside her wondered why that was necessary, but the woman inside her knew. There was something in Gray's eyes that called to her, seemed to devour her soul every time she looked at him. He scared her, he made her want to run and do everything she could to save herself.

Suzy realized that Claire was watching her, a knowing look in her eyes. Quickly putting up her defenses, Suzy did what she did best: bluffed. "Ugh, well, no biggie, I guess. Just another uptight geek to grace our presence here, right? I mean, why should it bother me? I haven't given him a thought since he was here annoying me last time. Maybe he will actually buy himself a pair of jeans or something, though. Those uptight, heavily starched suits are so depressing. He should really lay off the hair products. Do you think a hurricane could move that hair?" Suzy ended her tirade and grimaced as she looked at Claire. Okay, maybe she should have limited those comments to no more than two. She was rattled and, when that happened, the words kept flowing no matter how hard she tried to stop them. She was grateful that it was Claire, someone who would never judge her or try to peel the layers back to see what all the protests were hiding. Claire didn't have to, because she knew.

Years ago, Suzy had met Claire at Danvers International, where they both worked. Claire was the personal assistant to the company president and CEO, Jason Danvers, while Suzy handled all the many special events for Danvers. Two people couldn't be more opposite than the two women were, but their friendship worked. Suzy was loud and outgoing while Claire was quiet and thoughtful.

Claire wore her long auburn hair loose around her shoulders now; thank God, Suzy thought, she'd given up the ponytails and buns she used to wear. Suzy styled her long red hair to suit her mood. She also dressed to suit her moods, and leather and stiletto heels played a large role. Both were blessed to be a little above-average height, and, Suzy couldn't lie, she loved her own perky, plump boobs. If you could take half of each, they would make the perfect person.

It was so hard to believe that the person in front of her now was married to Jason, the CEO of Danvers, and pregnant with his child. The fairy tale had come true for Claire, and her Prince Charming had slain all of her dragons. Suzy couldn't think of anyone who deserved it more. After her sister and abusive father were killed in a car accident several years ago, Claire had struggled to support her ailing mother. When her mother suffered a stroke, her medication was altered and her recovery was miraculous. Now she lived down the beach from Claire in a house designed by Jason. Claire had given up her boring clothing and hairstyle she'd always favored, and now she practically glowed. She was still Jason's assistant, until after the baby was born. If Suzy were a person prone to crying, this story would certainly have her sobbing.

Claire reached over and covered Suzy's hand with her own. "Suz, it'll be fine. Gray really isn't that bad when you get to know him. I'm actually quite fond of him. His brother, Nicholas, will also be moving here to assist with the daily operations."

"Nicholas? Stuffed Shirt has a brother? God, please don't tell me he's smoking hot too!"

Laughing, Claire said, "Well, I don't know what you consider 'smoking,' but he's similar to Gray in coloring and he's quite good-looking. Not as good-looking as Jason, because no one looks that good, but well above average."

Looking at Claire in horror, Suzy sputtered out, "Geez, where do these guys come from? Jason, Gray, and now Nicholas. If he looks even half as good, every woman here will stay in heat."

"Every woman, Suz?"

"Um, well, not you, obviously. I mean, except for Jason. And not me; my head isn't turned by a good piece of eye candy, but, for sure, every other woman here."

Suzy knew that her friend wasn't fooled for a minute by all her protests, so she wisely decided to change the subject. Even as she asked all the right questions about Claire's new life, her mind was on a tall man with dark hair and compelling green eyes that seemed to see through all of her defenses. Suzy was deathly afraid that the battle to storm the walls to her heart had already begun.